I0762007

SEE HER GONE

(A Mia North FBI Suspense Thriller—Book 5)

Rylie Dark

Rylie Dark

Bestselling author Rylie Dark is author of the SADIE PRICE FBI SUSPENSE THRILLER series, comprising six books (and counting); the MIA NORTH FBI SUSPENSE THRILLER series, comprising six books (and counting); the CARLY SEE FBI SUSPENSE THRILLER, comprising six books (and counting); and the MORGAN STARK FBI SUSPENSE THRILLER, comprising three books (and counting).

An avid reader and lifelong fan of the mystery and thriller genres, Rylie loves to hear from you, so please feel free to visit www.ryliedark.com to learn more and stay in touch.

ISBN: 978-1-0943-9558-6

BOOKS BY RYLIE DARK

SADIE PRICE FBI SUSPENSE THRILLER

ONLY MURDER (Book #1)
ONLY RAGE (Book #2)
ONLY HIS (Book #3)
ONLY ONCE (Book #4)
ONLY SPITE (Book #5)
ONLY MADNESS (Book #6)

MIA NORTH FBI SUSPENSE THRILLER

SEE HER RUN (Book #1)
SEE HER HIDE (Book #2)
SEE HER SCREAM (Book #3)
SEE HER VANISH (Book #4)
SEE HER GONE (Book #5)
SEE HER DEAD (Book #6)

CARLY SEE FBI SUSPENSE THRILLER

NO WAY OUT (Book #1)
NO WAY BACK (Book #2)
NO WAY HOME (Book #3)
NO WAY LEFT (Book #4)
NO WAY UP (Book #5)
NO WAY TO DIE (Book #6)

MORGAN STARK FBI SUSPENSE THRILLER

TOO LATE (Book #1)
TOO CLOSE (Book #2)
TOO FAR GONE (Book #3)

CHAPTER ONE

Stars everywhere.

Merry Summerhill laid back against the battered old sofa in her trailer, her fingers losing their grip on the plunger of the syringe. At that moment, the moment she injected that liquid gold into her veins, nothing else mattered but those stars. She felt herself speeding into outer space like a rocket at full speed, like going into hyperspace in *Star Wars,* where everything seemed to blur around her.

The crash would come soon. Too soon. It came quicker, now. Meth had helped her to lose her flawless complexion, her smile, her job, her family, and most of her friends. But could she give it up? Did she even want to?

No.

She savored the feeling of weightlessness, caring about none of those things. She didn't even know what day it was, what time it was. Her shades were pulled low, as always. Merry hated the sunlight. She hated the outdoors, and with good reason.

There were people looking for her, out there.

Inside, she was safe. She had a gun, stashed in the coffee table, and she wasn't afraid to use it. Here, with her meth, she had everything she needed.

A moment later, the curtains moved, the stars had disappeared, and the urge was back. She wanted that next hit.

She scrambled off the sofa and looked at her stash. She'd gone through hell to get it. She found two sad, deflated bags with only a trace of the powder left.

Funny. She'd only just gotten them. How could she have nearly blown through it all? She couldn't remember when, how, or with whom.

Dammit, she thought. Mick was all the way at the other end of the town. And she probably wasn't his favorite person right now. She'd slept with him and all of his friends—nameless, faceless guys she wouldn't even know if she saw them in broad daylight— to earn a bag, but when they left, and she saw it all there, laid out in front of her, she was like a kid in a candy store. She'd taken two, figuring he had so many, he probably didn't count them.

But Mick wasn't an idiot. He was a businessman, first and foremost, so maybe he *did* count them. And he definitely wasn't the kind of person you wanted to piss off.

She shouldn't have done it. It was too big a risk.

But right then, she wished she'd taken *three* bags.

She leaned over the coffee table, trying to see if she could arrange enough of the white powder to give herself another hit. As she was trying to scrape it together, she heard tires, kicking up gravel in front of the house. The beam from headlights slashed across her line of vision.

Merry stood up, grabbed the gun, and went to the door, just as someone began to bang on it. "Merry! I know you're in there."

It was Mick.

She looked around at the two empty bags on the table. Quickly, she scooped them up and shoved them in a drawer, then went to the door.

"Merry!"

"Go away, Mick! I'm warning you . . ." she called out.

"I'm not leaving until I get my money!"

That was the truth. If Mick was anything, it was persistent. She wouldn't get rid of him until she gave him something.

She opened the door and smiled in response to his scowl. Mick looked scarier than usual, with his shaved head, tattooed neck, and red scar, running from temple to chin. His black eyes focused on her, his pierced lip curled into a snarl, and he held out a big hand, waiting for her to drop something into it.

"Hi," she said innocently, slapping his palm. "Are you looking for more fun?"

He scowled and ran his eye around the place. "Don't give me that bullshit. You took an extra bag from my stash. I want it back."

She widened her eyes innocently. "I don't know what you're talking about. I took one bag. And that's paid in full."

"Like hell you did. You took two. I know. I'd just counted them before you got there."

She tossed her blonde hair over her shoulder and folded her arms over her tank top. "If you're missing some, don't look at me. It must've been one of your friends—"

"It's you." He pushed open the door, shoving her out of the way, but she met him with the gun, pointing it at his chest.

"Get out."

He lifted his hands at once. "Hey. Watch it."

"*You* watch it!" she shouted, and he took a step back, then another, until he stumbled on the front steps. "I want you out of here!"

He shook his head. "I want my bag."

"I don't have it."

"You used it already? Then I want my money. Three hundred," he demanded.

She rolled her eyes. "I told you. I don't have—"

"I know you took it. And I'm expecting payback."

She cocked the gun. "Get out."

He looked at it and backed off. "This isn't over."

"Whatever," she said, rolling her eyes. She reached over and grabbed the door handle, pulling it shut.

Then she slumped against it. No, it wasn't over. He'd arrange some sort of payback, eventually, and the cost would be dear. She knew that.

Merry meandered back through the kitchen, grabbing a beer from the fridge before settling down on the sofa again. She twisted the cap and took a long swig, then opened the coffee table drawer and stared at the empty bags. Her hands shook, just as if she were going through withdrawal. It would get worse if she didn't find her next hit, soon. So bad that she couldn't sleep, eat, or think about anything other than the drug.

She was already getting there.

She pulled the baggy out and licked it greedily. All she tasted was plastic. The night seemed to stretch on before her, long, lonely, and empty.

When she was younger, in school and full of dreams for the future, she'd hoped to go to college to be a vet tech. She'd spent most of her teenage years babysitting all the young brats in the neighborhood, making money so that she could get a car, go to school, and make something of herself.

But she'd gone through all that cash she'd amassed in a matter of months.

All for the meth.

Now, she had nothing.

She'd heard of people who'd given their lives up for the drug, and Merry had promised her older sister, Shilah, who cared for her, that would never be her.

That promise seemed so long ago, made in another lifetime.

Nothing had gone according to that naïve, rose-colored-glasses plan of her teenage years. Shilah had gotten into her own troubles, and toted off to prison. She'd been stuck, watching Shilah's son Rocky, her nephew, and he and the other kids she was babysitting, were a handful. Holding down a babysitting business and taking care of a headstrong twelve-year-old boy hadn't exactly been her idea of easy. The only time she ever got reprieve was when he'd hole up in his bedroom to satisfy either his porn or video-game addiction—she didn't care which, because it allowed her to be alone.

And then her boyfriend—that loser, Dirk— introduced her to something that would take the edge off.

She'd used only occasionally, up until Shilah got out of prison and Rocky moved out to live back with her. Then, it was to take the edge off. Gradually, though, it became every night. Dirk provided everything she needed—for free. But then, Dirk went and cheated on her with her best friend, Amanda, and then that girl Lily at the bar. After having her own dalliances with other men, fighting every night, she eventually kicked Dirk out. Then she found out pretty quickly how expensive her habit was. Now, in a matter of a couple months, here she was, penniless, friendless, hopeless . . . and at the absolute bottom of the hole she'd been digging herself into over the past three years, since graduation.

Merry, you're an addict. You need to get help.

Crumpling the bag up, she threw it down in disgust. She couldn't live like this anymore.

Sliding off the couch, she decided right then and there that this was enough. Grabbing the beer, she went to the sink and emptied it down the drain.

That was when she heard the sound.

A scratching, coming from inside her bedroom. It sounded like someone was trying to pry open the screen on the window.

She swallowed. "Rocky?" she called, but there was no answer.

No, it can't be Rocky. The little horndog's been back with his momma ever since she got out of the pen. And she doesn't work tonight. Try again.

Her heart leapt into her throat, until the realization dawned.

Mick.

Of course. He wasn't going to let her go this easily. She should've known he'd try to get back at her tonight, probably by sneaking up on her and roughing her up when she least expected it.

You're not nearly as crafty as you think you are, Mick, she thought, grabbing the gun and creeping down the hallway. *I heard you a mile away.*

Holding the gun at the ready, she inched her way to the door of her room and pushed it open, expecting to see him weaseling his way through the window.

But he wasn't there.

The window was gaping open, the thin muslin curtains billowing in the breeze. It'd been closed before, but there was no one there now.

Confused, she reached for the light switch. But she never got there. A form was looming right in front of it, large and imposing. Between them, like a flash of white-hot lightning, a blade gleamed. Before she could even think to aim her gun, the figure plunged the full of the knife into her middle. She felt the skin giving way, the searing pain, the scrape of the metal against her rib bones, and when she looked down, she could feel the warm blood, spreading over her center.

Her vision wavered and bent as she tried to blink some sense into what had just happened. This time, as she fell to her knees, she saw stars of a different kind, more beautiful and brilliant than she'd ever seen before.

And then, nothing.

CHAPTER TWO

"Don't move," Mia North breathed into the ear of the politician she hated. "Don't even breathe."

To drive her point home, she pressed the point of the letter opener deeper into Wilson Andrews's throat. He gripped the arms of his leather office chair. His Adam's apple bobbed.

The sound of the sirens outside drew closer. From here, she could see their red and blue lights, bouncing off the panels of the vertical blinds at the window behind his desk.

She was trapped.

"Don't do anything stupid," he murmured, his head pressed back against the chair, fighting to keep as far away as possible from the weapon. He was nervous. And he *should* be.

After all, he'd put her through the ringer over the past nine months, putting her through every hell imaginable. She'd been arrested for a murder she didn't commit, convicted, and was now on the run, top of the list of Most Wanted Criminals in the Dallas area. She'd been ripped from her family, her husband and daughter, Kelsey. So a little payback wouldn't be out of the question.

Or even a lot.

And it would be so easy to end his life like that. Just a little pressure, and the man who'd ruined her life would be gone forever.

But she couldn't. Unlike Wilson Andrews, she had morals. Though Mia had been relieved of her FBI badge months ago, she still abided by their standards. Wilson Andrews, on the other hand, had his sights set on the State Senate, and was prepared to remove whatever obstacles were in his way, by whatever means necessary—theft, blackmail, coercion, and yes, even murder. The man wasn't worth anything. The world would be better off without him.

And yet, her hand shook as she looked down at the point of the letter opener, pressed against his throat. The pounding footsteps outside his office told her the police were getting closer. She took a deep breath and scanned her surroundings. The window behind her was open, the blinds swaying in the breeze. It looked like a large enough gap to slip through. But what was beyond it?

She didn't know. But at the moment, it was her only chance of escape.

"You're screwed. You're going to prison for a long time." A smile crept onto Wilson Andrews's face. He was always so ineffably smug, even at his worst moments. After all the sinister tricks he'd pulled, he wasn't worried in the least. He knew he was untouchable.

She'd always wanted to pull him down a few pegs. But never in her life had she wanted it so much. She pressed harder, and a bead of blood appeared at the point of her weapon.

He winced, and then he smiled. "A shame, really. I admire your fortitude. And I can't say my trail's been completely clean. Mistakes were made. Maybe if you'd taken another look at that cold case I was nearly attached to, you would've seen that. Instead, you'll rot in jail, while I'll become the next senator of this great state of Texas."

Pompous slimeball. Gritting her teeth, she made the decision right then: She'd never let Wilson Andrews get his way. Even if it killed her.

Just then, there was a crash against the door. Another crash. The police were breaking it down.

The third try, the door gave way, and the police burst in, guns drawn. The three officers assessed the situation in a split second, and the barrels of their guns turned toward her. "Drop it!" they announced.

Without hesitation, Mia backed away, still behind Wilson Andrews's large executive office chair to give her cover. She climbed onto the ledge of the window and climbed out. There, she found a small ledge. She noticed a downspout and a vertical column on either side that was part of the building's architectural design. She shimmied around it, just as the police arrived at the window.

"Where'd she go?" she heard one of them say as she pressed herself against the brick side of the building.

"She must've fallen there. I think I see here there. In the bushes!" the other said, and they pushed away from the window and their voices trailed off. In the commotion, she heard Wilson Andrews's voice, far away, and annoyed. "Get her! Don't let her get away, idiots!"

At that moment, she swore she'd get away, no matter what she had to do.

She grabbed ahold of the downspout. More police cars were arriving, the officers beginning to congregate on her side of the building. It was only a matter of time before they shined a spotlight on the facade of the building and found her.

She couldn't go one floor down to the ground, or they'd find her. Looking up, she decided that was her only chance.

Luckily, she'd had plenty of climbing training at Quantico, and the downspout's brackets attaching it to the side of the building were perfect footholds. She scaled the side of the wall like an insect and threw a leg over the top lip of the edifice. As she began to steal across the flat roof, she heard the beating of helicopter rotors.

She looked up, spotting its lights in the dark sky. Of course, they'd pull out all the stops for their beloved Wilson Andrews, Dallas's golden boy. What next? Calling in the National Guard?

If only they knew him the way I know him, she thought as she crouched behind a chimney, looking for her next move.

She skirted around the periphery of the rooftop, stopping every so often to look over and gauge her opportunity to get out. Finally, when she reached the back of the building, she saw another downspout, leading to a line of bushes. Beyond that, across a slim patch of lawn and landscaping, there was a thick, dark forest. If she could just make it down the side of the building, she could be lost in that forest, and escape.

In no time, she grabbed the top of the downspout and scuttled down it, half sliding, using her toes pressed up against the brick to stop herself from falling too fast. As she made it down, sweat poured down her temples, feeling icy against her skin in the cool evening breeze. She heard the shouts of the police officers, so nearby, which urged her to go faster.

When she was between the second and first floors, she looked down. Another shout made her lose her concentration entirely, and she let go of the pipe. She tried to grab it, but her sweat-slicked fingers lost their grasp and she wound up falling back.

A second later, she landed in the inadequate cushion of an evergreen bush, the branches scraping her face and arms. She pulled herself up, disentangling herself from its brambles and, taking a quick look to her right and left, raced as fast as she could for the tree line.

She made it just as a spotlight beam from the helicopter arced across the lawn she'd just crossed.

Crouching there, catching her breath, she watched as police officers finally began to walk around the back of the building, searching for her.

She couldn't stay there. They'd soon fan out and try to cover the surrounding forest as well.

I can't say my trail's been completely clean. Mistakes were made. Maybe if you'd taken another look at that cold case I was nearly attached to, you would've seen that. Instead, you'll rot in jail, while I'll become the next senator of this great state of Texas.

Thinking of those words, she skipped into a run, navigating around the forms of trees, unsure as to where her path would lead. Wherever it led, it meant one thing: As long as she was outside, she had a hope. Hope that she could nail Wilson Andrews for his crimes and prove he'd framed her to cover them up.

She'd been given another chance. And now was the time to act upon this information.

CHAPTER THREE

It was near morning before Mia finally emerged from the forest, finding herself in an established neighborhood with modest, seventies-style, split-level homes and mature trees. As she came up to the chain link fence surrounding a lawn full with a swing set and trampoline, a drooling pit bull raced up and started to bark viciously at her.

Backing away, she hurried along the fence until the dog was out of view, to another home with no fence. She hurried down the street, finally stopping at a 7-Eleven store to catch her breath.

That was too close. She really had to lie low, now.

That was another problem. She wanted to just run off someplace where no one would recognize her, but she was so thirsty, she could barely think.

And now, she was in trouble once again. She'd left her car outside Andrews's place, parked a distance away, but it definitely wasn't safe to go back yet. She'd left her bag in there, too, with most of her money and her belongings.

Once again, she'd lost it all. It seemed like she was constantly having to start from square one.

Reaching into her pockets, she pulled out her phone and a crumpled five-dollar bill.

Perfect. That wasn't going to get her very far.

She needed help. But her list of allies had been growing thin. Her husband, her sister Francine, her partner David Hunter . . . she'd involved all of them, recently, to help her out when she was in a pinch. And she'd endangered them in the process. She couldn't do that again.

If she was going to get out of this latest pinch, she'd need help from someone else.

But who?

She ran down a mental list of people she knew, but none of them seemed like good options. Sighing, she pulled up the hood on her jacket to cover much of her face, and went inside the convenience store.

The store was empty, except for the clerk behind the counter and a pregnant woman with a young baby on her hip, who was standing in front of a diaper display. As she stepped in, the pregnant woman smiled at her. She went to the back of the store, grabbed a cherry Sports drink from the refrigerated case, and then went to the snacks aisle. *What great breakfast am I going to use my last five dollars on?*

As she stood there, her mind went to what Wilson Andrews had said to her.

I can't say my trail's been completely clean. Mistakes were made. Maybe if you'd taken another look at that cold case I was nearly attached to, you would've seen that . . .

What did he mean by that? What cold case?

The truth was, though the media liked to paint him as an angel who could do no wrong, Wilson Andrews had been tied to a number of criminal cases. But he'd always emerged from them, without even a ding to his record. Even the case she'd investigated, about the missing girl Sara Waverly, which had been perpetrated by Jerry Andrews . . . his fans had quickly forgotten about his role in covering it up.

That case wasn't cold, though. It had been solved. So was there another case? She'd have to look into it.

Easier said than done. Being on the run meant she had no access to the files she used to easily be able to call up on her computer.

The only person who could look into it for her was her partner, David Hunter.

It was a gamble. But weeks ago, when she'd first escaped, she and David had arranged a place to get notes and information to one another. It was an abandoned auto body shop that had a night drop box. She hadn't been able to check it in a while. Now seemed as good a time as any.

The only problem was that it was on the other side of town.

Grabbing a sleeve of donuts, she went to the front of the store. She gnawed on her lip as she laid her purchases on the counter, thinking. She'd have to try to hitch a ride somehow, without calling too much attention to herself.

"That'll be $5.80," the cashier, a portly twenty-something guy with a scraggly beard said, disinterestedly.

Mia blinked. "For a Sports drink and some donuts?"

He nodded. "Yep."

"That's a lot."

He shrugged. "Inflation. Hey, I don't make the prices."

She looked down at the five-dollar bill in her hand and grimaced. Then she started to look behind her and realized someone else was in line, waiting to check out. Great. The last thing she needed was to call attention to herself.

The cashier sighed and tapped his fingers on the side of the register, waiting.

She set the five dollar bill down and said, “Forget the donuts. I’ll—”

“Oh, nonsense,” a female voice said behind her, and a credit card was plunked next to her money. “You got to eat. Skinny thing like you.”

She looked up to see the pregnant woman, balancing the toddler on her hip, a basket and her purse on the other arm. She had her hair piled on her head and was wearing a long, maxi tank dress. Grinning, she said to the cashier, “Honey, just put the whole thing on that card. And this stuff, too.”

She motioned to her basket. Quickly, Mia helped take the basket full of diapers and a teething ring from the belabored mother and set it on the counter. “Oh, thank you. But I should—”

“Don’t worry, Honey. Pay it forward.” The card was swiped and the purchases bought, making it too late to argue.

“Thank you,” Mia said meekly, taking the bag of diapers and handing it to the woman. She took her snack from the counter and followed the woman out, opening the door to let the woman through. “I will.”

“Aw, Sweetheart. I know when life gets tough. I’ve been there,” she said, stopping in front of her Mercedes to power open the locks. She easily pulled open the back door and started to put her child inside. “It isn’t easy. But you keep your chin up. Good things will come!”

“Thank you,” she said, wandering out to the parking lot, hoping to hitch a ride at a gas station she thought was nearby, which was popular with truckers.

“Wait, Hon,” the woman said when she finished strapping in her child. “You gonna be okay? You need some help?”

Mia stopped, considering. “Well, I—”

“Come on, Honey,” she said, reaching into her purse and handing her a twenty. “Here you go. Take this. You need to look after yourself. When life gives you lemons, you make lemonade. You have a job? A place to stay?”

Mia said, “I’m in between places right now, actually. My family—”

“Oh . . . you’re trying to get back to your family? Are they close? Can I give you a ride?”

Mia nodded. That was exactly what she was hoping to hear. “That would be great.”

“Sure, hop in,” she said, opening her door and carefully sliding her large belly under the steering column. Mia went around to the passenger side and saw the FALLON FOR STATE SENATE sticker on the back bumper.

Erica Fallon. One of Wilson Andrews’s challengers in the upcoming senate race. Mia had to smile. She already liked the young mother for helping her out when she needed it, but now, she really *liked* her.

Mia got in, giving a quick thumbs up to the little kid in the car seat in back, who was wearing a striped red-white-and-blue jumper and sucking on a blue raspberry slushy. The woman put her key in the ignition and noticed her looking. “That’s Charlie, my first. You have any kids?”

As the woman pulled out, Mia nodded, her heart hurting at the thought of Kelsey. Her daughter was nine. She hadn’t been a mother to Kelsey in months, ever since her arrest. “One. A daughter.”

“Oh.” The woman reached across the center console and patted her knee. “Haven’t seen her in a while, hmm?”

Mia looked at her in surprise.

“I can tell,” she went on, navigating to the exit. “You don’t just look starved for food. You look like you could use the love, too. So where to?”

Her first instinct was to tell the woman her home address. She desperately wanted to go back. But she’d endangered them all enough as it was. She couldn’t.

So the abandoned auto body shop it was.

There was a condo complex on that highway, separated by an overpass. If she was dropped off there, she could easily navigate to the shop. “The Swiftwater Estates,” she said. “On Briar Ave. If it’s not too much trouble?”

“Oh. I know it,” the woman said with a smile. “No trouble at all. Sit back and relax, and enjoy your meal, and I’ll have you there in no time.”

She took off, headed for the condos, and as she drove, she played a children's CD for Charlie, with "Head, Shoulders, Knees and Toes" and "I'm Bringing Home a Baby Bumblebee," much to the child's delight, since he kept singing every word and laughing. It made Mia smile, too.

As Mia took a swig from her Sports drink, the mother said, "So you were on your way home, huh? Where have you been all this time?"

Mia didn't want to answer. She knew she'd have to lie, and the less she said, the better. "I was traveling, and I lost all my things," she said, opening the package of donuts.

It wasn't a lie.

"Oh, that's terrible. Do you want to file a police report or—"

"I'll do that later," she said quickly, and then swiftly changed the subject. "So you think Fallon's going to pull it out this November?"

The woman shrugged. "Oh. I don't know. I sure hope so. It's better than the alternative. That Andrews is a creep, in my opinion."

"Is he?" she asked innocently as she nibbled at a powdered donut. She had to know more. Most everyone in the state of Texas seemed to think he was the second coming.

"Oh, yeah, he's all sorts of shady!" she said, rolling her eyes. "Typical politician, can't believe a word he says. And I mean, that whole scandal with him covering up for his brother, who'd kidnapped those girls? I think he knew way more than he's letting on."

"You do?" Mia asked, surprised. So there were people out there who were on her side.

"Oh, sure. The media's so far up his butt, they'd never challenge him. But they're brothers, cut from the same cloth. I wouldn't be surprised if Wilson Andrews helped his brother kidnap those girls. But is anyone looking into it? Of course not." She shook her head. "I wouldn't vote for that scum-sucking liar if he was the only candidate on the ballot."

Mia nodded. "I agree."

They pulled up at the Swiftwater Estates, a series of four boxy high-rise buildings with dull gray siding. "Anywhere I should park you?" the woman asked.

"Right here is good," Mia said as she pulled to the curb. She grabbed the handle. "Thanks."

"No problem, girl. Oh!" She reached into the console and pulled out a pink business card, which she handed to Mia. It said:

Ravishing Nails

Randi Willis, Owner

Her phone number and an address south of the city was written underneath.

"That's me," she said proudly, showing off her own patterned manicure. "I do nail parties for people in my neighborhood, if you're ever interested."

Mia looked down at her own ragged fingernails and blushed.

"Of course," the woman, Randi, said with a blush. "That's not why I'm giving you my card. It's in case you need me, for anything. A ride somewhere, a few dollars, or just to talk. I'm here!"

"Thank you, Randi," Mia said with a nod as she stepped out.

She went to close the door, and Randi said, "Of course, we girls need to stick together! But oh—" Mia bristled as the woman's tone changed from friendly to warning. "I just realized . . . I don't know your name?"

"Sue," she said, using a name she'd used in the past, when asked the question.

"Okay, Sue! Have a good one!" She drove off, cheerfully beeping as she did, the little boy in the back seat waving feverishly.

Mia finished up her Sports drink and decided to save a few of the donuts for later. Folding the bag over, she watched the young mother speed off down the driveway. When the Mercedes pulled out of sight, Mia hurried across the grassy area separating the condo property from the abandoned auto shop. Leaping across a small gully, she climbed the embankment and jogged over to the front garage bays, checking carefully around her to make sure no one was nearby.

Whenever David communicated with her, he usually put a rather large craft paper envelope in the drop box, which she could easily grab. They'd been using this method of communication to discuss any new leads they found on her case, anything that might be helpful to finally prove her innocence.

But when she reached in, she found nothing.

That meant no news. Either that, or David hadn't been able to get away. The U.S. Marshals and their higher-ups at the FBI had been tightening a noose on her former partner, making it difficult for him to do any legwork on her behalf.

Maybe they were on to him. Maybe it was a danger for her to even be here.

Still, she had to try. She had to leave him a note about what she'd learned from Wilson Andrews, to ask him to go back into the files and see if there were any other cases that he might've been implicated in.

But then, it hit her. She had no paper, no pen. Nothing to create the note.

Heaving a sigh of disappointment, she thunked her head with the heel of her hand. If she was smart, she would've asked Randi for something to write with. She looked around helplessly, then spotted a small red child's crayon on the ground.

It was better than nothing.

She tore a piece of paper from the white paper bag the donuts had come in, and wrote:

D- WA mentioned cold case he made mistakes in. Pls look into old cold cases he was involved in. Thx- M

She wanted to write more, about how she was and where she was headed. She figured he'd want to know, just as she was dying to know what was going on in his world. But by then, the point on the crayon was so dull that most of the words bled together. She hoped he'd be able to read it. She quickly folded it and stuck her hand into the drop box, hoping he'd be able to find the small piece of wrinkled scrap paper in the confines of the giant metal box.

But as she was setting it inside, her fingertips grazed another slip of paper.

Her heart skipped a beat as she fished it out. It was an index card, folded in half. The word MIA was written on it, but it didn't look like David's handwriting.

Her spine straightened, and she scanned the area again. Did someone else know about their secret place? If so, how?

Seeing no one, she opened up the piece of paper and was greeted by a letter, written in very small print. This *definitely* wasn't David's doing. She read:

Dear Mia,

I hope you get this. Sorry but I had no other way of getting in touch. I spoke with your partner and he said he would get this to you.

I need your help. If you can meet me, I'll be at the Coco Café in Morning Star shopping mall at 10 am on the 5th. Please come. You are my last resort.

Shilah Summerhill

Mia stared at the message for a long time. Shilah Summerhill. The name sparked recognition in her at once. Shilah had been her cellmate in the Women's Correctional Facility, during the trial, before she was scheduled to be moved out to New Mexico. The woman was brash, large, and sarcastic, but Mia had loved her. She'd kept Mia sane during all those lonely nights in prison, as she'd been her only friend. If it hadn't been for Shilah, who knew where Mia would've been?

Something was clearly wrong. From what Mia remembered during their evening chats as they lay in their bunks, talking about everything, Shilah had been set to be released from prison. This stint of hers had been related to forging a couple of checks. So she'd gotten out, and likely gone home to her boy, Rocky. Had something happened? Why did Shilah need her, a woman who was wanted for murder? What could she possibly do to help?

All Mia knew was that she couldn't say no. As dangerous as it was to meet with anyone around here, Shilah had been there during her time of need. Shilah had stood up for her when Angel Vasquez, a criminal Mia had put in jail, had come after her.

She owed Shilah her life.

So she would be there. No matter what.

She checked her phone. The fifth was today. The Coco Café wasn't in the greatest section of town, but if she started walking now, she could probably be there in an hour.

She checked her phone again for the time. That meant that she would get there . . .

Late.

Really late.

It was five of ten *right now.* And if she missed Shilah, she probably wouldn't get another chance.

It was risky to hitchhike on this road, so close to home. She'd be wasting time trying to find a ride that could be better spent running.

She took a deep breath. *Nothing like a little morning exercise.*

As she was about to break into a run, she realized there was something else scribbled on the back of the index card. This *was* in David's handwriting: *Nothing new to report. - D*

It was just as she thought. She knew he was trying, but his hands were largely tied. He had their supervisor, Pembroke, breathing down his neck, not to mention that Marshal, Kane Wilcox, also on the case.

She felt guilty for even asking him to keep her apprised of anything new. He'd gone above and beyond for her.

Tucking the card into the pocket of her jeans, she rushed off in the direction of the Coco Café, hoping Shilah hadn't left yet.

CHAPTER FOUR

By taking the backroads and cutting across parking lots with her hood pulled tight around her face, Mia managed to make it to Coco Café at 10:35.

Pulling up the hood of her jacket, she went in and looked around.

No Shilah.

Sighing, she ordered a small coffee with the twenty dollars she'd gotten from Randi, and sat in a small booth in the corner, on the off chance she came back. After that run, she needed the rest.

A few moments later, she saw Shilah, lumbering across the parking lot, and her eyes lit up. Shilah was a big woman, shaped like a barrel, with close-cropped dark hair and a perpetual sly smile. The last time Mia had seen her, they were all dressed in the Correctional Facility's fashionable orange uniform. Now, Shilah was wearing a giant T-shirt with the Nike symbol emblazoned on the front, capri workout pants, and flip flops. She shuffled to the entrance, opened the door, and stepped inside, heading for the counter.

Though she was a considerable distance away, Mia could hear her every word—the woman's voice carried. "Chai latte, extra cream, and I'll take three of those," she said, pointing at the case.

Mia was pressed against the wall, hood on, trying to be small and unnoticeable. But she was prepared to wave at Shilah when she turned around. It turned out, though, that she didn't have to. When she collected her food, Shilah headed straight toward Mia, as if she'd always known she was there.

Maybe I'm not doing such a good job at flying under the radar, Mia wondered as her friend lowered herself into the chair across from Mia.

"You came back?"

"Yeah, I thought you might be running late, with all your *engagements*. Long time no see," Shilah said with a wink.

"You recognize me?"

Shilah snorted, and lowered her voice. "You look guilty, girl. You're the only one in the place who looks like they have something to hide. Loosen up."

Mia looked around and straightened as she caught a glimpse of her reflection in a mirror across the café. She was hunched over, her hood covering most of her face, like some comical dark figure from a children's movie. Shilah was probably right. She was probably overdoing it. She loosened her hood, but didn't pull it back. "Sorry, I've never done this before."

Shilah laughed. "Seems to me like you're doing a pretty good job. People round here are going crazy trying to find you."

Mia nodded. "It hasn't been easy."

"I'll bet. I've been reading up on you. The stories I hear!" She banged the table with a hand and then reached for the first of three bear claws she'd bought, taking a huge bite. "Have you been able to find anything out about that politician that screwed you over?"

She shook her head. "Very little. But I'm working on it."

"I pray every day that you find something so you can go on back to that little girl of yours. Have you seen her?"

"Once or twice. For a few moments. But obviously . . ." Tears sprang to her eyes, and she blinked furiously, trying to hold them back. That was the last thing she wanted to do now. "So, I obviously got your note. What is this about? Everything's been okay since you got out, hasn't it?"

She nodded. "It was. I got out a month ago. Got my Rocky back. Moved back into my place, got a job. Everything was going well, and I really felt like things were going to be good. But then . . ." She let out a sigh.

"Something bad happened?" Mia prompted, sipping her coffee. "To Rocky?"

"No. Not Rocky. My little sister. Merry. I told you about her, remember?"

Mia remembered. "Yes. She was the one looking after Rocky while you were in jail, right?"

"That's right. She was only twenty-four. She loved animals. Had her whole life ahead of her." Her smile fell from her lips, and she took another bite of her pastry.

"*Was*?"

"She was murdered. Two days ago. Stabbed in the stomach and left there, to bleed. When I found her, the next morning, it was too late."

Mia gasped and patted her chest. "I'm so sorry. That's so awful. Did they catch who did it?"

She ran a hand through her scrubby hair and shook her head. "No clue."

"Do you have any idea?"

"No. She was mixed up with some bad people, though, I think. She was trying to get her life in order but every time she did, something held her back. I had enough to deal with on my own, trying to get a job and take care of Rocky, so I can't say I was there for her, even after I got out of the pen. So I don't know what happened or who she was dealing with in those last days."

"What did the police say?"

"Nothin'," she shrugged.

"They said nothing?" Mia found that a little hard to believe. Every crime scene she'd ever been to, the police descended upon it like ants on a cookie. "How can that be?"

"Because they don't like our kind. They stay away."

Our kind. Now Mia understood. Mia was used to living in the upscale area of town. But she didn't have to travel there to know the police catered to the more well-off. In the poorer sections of town, that wasn't the case. It was a sad reality of life. "They closed the case already?"

She nodded.

"Without finding a killer?"

Shilah shrugged. "The people in the trailer park are all pretty closed off and don't like the police poking around. And the police won't bother with it. They don't care. They just chalked it up to some druggie getting what was coming to her by her dealer, end of story. Case closed."

Mia listened and shook her head. It was true, in the worst of neighborhoods, the police were spread thin. They didn't have time to devote to these cases. "Was Merry . . ."

"A druggie?" Shilah nodded. "She had a loser boyfriend who was a dealer. And she tried to keep it together for Rocky. But when I took Rocky back and she broke up with that guy, I think it got worse. She was all alone."

"I'm really sorry. But I don't see how—"

"Rocky and I live on the other side of the park. And we think someone there is responsible for whatever happened. I want to find out who did it. I think it was someone in the park, and I don't want the same thing happening to my Rocky. I worry night and day about him."

"I see. But—"

"And now that Merry's gone, he's not gonna have anyone in the trailer park to call when I work nights. It's too dangerous for him. He has no one." Tears appeared in her eyes. "I don't got no one else to help me. So I thought of you. I found your partner and he told me he'd get this message to you."

"Yes . . ." Mia said, eyes narrowing. She knew where this was heading, but she didn't see how she could be involved. "I understand that. But—"

"Well, don't you get it? The police won't touch the place. They refuse. It's far outside of town, in no man's land. I own my trailer, and the one Merry was living in. If you stayed with me, you'd be safe. Everyone there sticks to their business. No one would even suspect, and if they did . . . well, they all got their own skeletons. I'm telling you, there's not a place in this city where you'd be safer. You can just come and pretend to be one of my cousins from out west, and no one'll be the wiser. Trust me."

Mia stared at her, trying to absorb the news. She'd wanted something like that. A place where she could be near the Wilson Andrews action, but stay out of the police's way. But it sounded too good to be true. "So you want me to try to find out who killed your sister?"

"If you could. You know things like that. With your FBI training and stuff. And I don't want Merry to have died in vain. I want her killer found." She popped the last of the pastry into her mouth and started to lick her fingers.

"Yes, maybe. But if the police are—"

"Trust me. They don't want to touch our place. You'd be safe."

Mia hesitated. It sounded good. Especially since right now, she had eighteen dollars to her name, no car, no place to stay, and grim prospects of getting out of town on her own. If she could just lie low for a little while in the trailer park, maybe she would have a chance to build up her resources again.

Shilah had said Mia was her last resort . . . but to Mia, it felt like Shilah was her last resort, too.

She nodded. "All right. Let's do it."

Shilah clapped her hands together. "Perfect," she said. "Should we go now?"

Mia nodded. She'd learned early on that the best way to avoid detection was to keep moving. She'd already spent too much time in this place, and was starting to get antsy, feeling like everyone was looking at her. "Yeah, let's go."

Shilah pulled her enormous stomach out from under the table, grabbed her trash, and tossed it in the can as Mia followed. When they stepped outside and toward a beaten Chevy truck, Shilah said, "You'll see, this'll be a good thing!"

Mia nodded, pushing back the many worries swirling in her head. If this was heading where she thought it was heading, that meant that in addition to going up against Wilson Andrews, now, she was also going to be taking on some drug dealers. And in her experience, some of them, with their vast networks and important friends, could be even more dangerous.

I hope you're right.

CHAPTER FIVE

In the late afternoon, David Hunter sat at his desk, sipping his fifth cup of coffee for the day and thinking about what the hell Mia North had gotten him into.

He thought about her often, but even more so, now. For the past few months, he'd had no idea where she was, most of the time. But if she'd been to the auto body shop lately, then he knew exactly where she was, right now.

The Coco Café, with a woman named Shilah Summerhill. Above all, Mia always had a desire to help. So if Shilah's story was right and they'd been close while in prison, then Mia would be there.

He hadn't thought much of the woman when she arrived at his office, a few days ago. Large, sloppy, oily-faced and missing a front eye-tooth, she'd more than let herself go. She'd filled his small office with the stench of body odor. After the fact, he'd looked her up and found out she was a small-time thief, who'd passed a few bad checks that had put her in prison for a short stint around the same time Mia was going through her ordeal. So he'd had no reason to want to help her.

And yet, like Mia, this woman had clearly been at the end of her rope. She needed help. And when she mentioned that Mia was her friend, he decided that he'd have to give Mia the option.

Now, he imagined the two of them, sipping coffee and discussing the murder of one Merry Summerhill. David had also looked into that case, but he hadn't found much—the police had done a cursory investigation and chalked it up to another casualty of the raging drug war in that rough neighborhood. *Nothing to see here, folks.* A shame, really, but with crime exploding in the resort town of Gun Springs City, law enforcement lacked the manpower to devote any real time to it.

Knowing Mia, she'd be compelled to help. She always did.

So that meant, right about now, Mia North was planning to go to Gun Springs City, east of Dallas. He had to admit, she had balls. Law enforcement was probably crawling all over that place, considering all the crime. Then again, it could've been genius. After all, there was no better way for a needle to hide itself than within a pile of other needles..

Either way, it was risky. But Mia was known for taking risks. Tackling Wilson Andrews at his home base? Confronting him? That was a foolish move, if ever he'd heard one. But it also sounded like the move of someone who wanted to bring all of this to an end. Mia had poked her head out in a big way, with that stunt.

Now, if she wanted not to get caught, she'd have to draw back in, go into hiding.

But she wasn't going to do that. Not now.

And that was the problem. If she kept going, and it was found out that he'd been helping her, he'd be sunk.

As he was contemplating this, someone knocked on his door, a quick rap. Expecting Pembroke, his supervisor, he was surprised to find U.S. Marshal Kane Wilcox there.

He rolled his eyes. "Agent."

The older man strolled in as if he owned the place, grinning. He sat down across from David without being invited and crossed one leg over the other. "Agent Hunter. That's no way to greet an old friend."

David's eyes narrowed. "Because I don't know why you're harassing me. I told you—"

"I don't call stopping by once or twice to say hello harassing, necessarily." He glanced down at his fingernails, flicked something from one of them, and then his eyes locked on the junior agent's. "Besides, you told me you'd let me know if you heard anything more, where Mia was concerned."

"That's right. I told you I'd be in touch if I heard anything more about Mia. And I haven't," he said. "I haven't heard from her in weeks, and I have no idea where she is. So you can—"

"I don't think that's true," he said, leaning forward. "I think you have a very good idea where she is. After her little stunt at the business of that senator?"

"I haven't been paying attention."

"No?" the Marshal's face was practically dripping with doubt.

David leaned back in his chair, meeting the man's gaze. But then he broke it. He had a feeling someone was on his tail, the last time he'd gone to deliver the message. He'd done some fancy evasion maneuvers, straight out of the FBI playbook, to lose whoever it was, and though he'd made sure no one was watching him, the mere act of evading anyone who could've been following him was suspicious enough. "Have you been following me, Agent?"

He smiled. "A bit. Here and there."

David frowned. He knew they were monitoring his comings and goings. They had his phone records, and monitored what he did in the office. He'd even gotten the feeling someone was watching him while he sat in the bleachers at his son Louie's baseball game. It was enough to make anyone paranoid, but David Hunter was worse than that, because he actually had something to hide. "What do you want? You should know by now that I'm not giving you anything where Mia North is concerned."

Agent Kane Wilcox ran his hands through his scrubby, salt-and-pepper hair, and smiled. "I know that. I can understand. After all, it was your testimony that put her away. You're feeling guilty about that, right?"

He stared at the man, stone-faced.

"You've had second thoughts, thinking maybe you pegged her wrong. Thinking maybe she didn't kill Ellis Horvath over some mad revenge scheme, after all."

Under the desk, David's hands tightened into fists. It was all true. Ellis Horvath was a true slimeball, and had been following Mia's daughter Kelsey around town, making threats. If she'd taken him out, he wouldn't blame her. But as an FBI agent, she had certain protocols to follow, and the evidence showed she'd acted with malice, shooting him while he was unarmed and unthreatening. David's testimony had been the truth—Mia North behaved impulsively, and with a lot of passion. But that had made her look rash, vengeful, and ultimately, guilty of cold-blooded murder.

"So what?"

Wilcox smiled. "Maybe I'm starting to come around to your point of view. Maybe I don't think Mia North is as guilty as they say, either."

David raised an eyebrow, studying him. "Bullshit."

"It's true. I think there's a lot more to it, and I want a chance to speak to her, to hear her side of the story."

"*Definite* bullshit. You want a chance to snap cuffs on her and bring her in, mark another notch on your belt. That's all," he said, shaking his head. "I may not be one of you, but I know how the Marshals work."

"I'm being honest with you," he said, his voice changing, becoming softer, more earnest. "On my word."

David scoffed. “You mean to tell me that you don’t want to capture the target you’ve been fighting tooth and nail to reel in for months. That you just want to talk? I don’t buy it.”

Wilcox shrugged. “Look. I know it sounds unbelievable. And yes, I’ve been following her a long time. I know she was key in solving those cases. The Andrews case. The one at the high school. The one at that cult in the desert down South. All of them. So that means she’s still hanging around here. And I don’t think she’s doing that because she wants to get caught. I think she’s here for one reason: because she’s trying to find out what really happened with Ellis Horvath, and clear her name.”

David stared at him. They’d spoken of this before, briefly, but he’d managed to throw the man off his back. At least, he’d thought. Now, the U.S. Marshal was back and refusing to take no for an answer.

The agent seemed sincere, but David still didn’t buy it. Marshals used every dirty trick in the book in order to gain information, in order to make their subjects trust them. So he wasn’t about to budge. No matter what. He wasn’t going to be the one to fail Mia North for a second time.

“Sorry,” David said, turning back to his computer. “I can’t help you.”

He stood up and shrugged. “A shame. Because Mia’s little jaunt is coming to an end. We know she’s in the area and we’re closing in on her. It’s only a matter of time before she’s in custody, and she rots in jail for the rest of her life.” He leaned forward and his grin widened. “So it turns out, I am the only one who can help her.”

David met his eyes and crossed his arms over his chest. Was that true? Things moved fast—after her little stunt at Andrews’s place, it made sense that things might’ve started to unravel. They might’ve been right on her tail. And he did know that if she was caught, there’d be no arguing her way out of it—she’d never get out. Her only hope now was finding out what really had happened to Ellis Horvath, and who had framed her for his murder.

He swallowed and pushed on his desk, rising to his feet, hoping to stare Wilcox down and feel more powerful. But the two men were of even height. “How do I know I can trust you?”

“You don’t, really,” Wilcox said with a shrug, straightening the pencil holder and tissue box on the top of David’s desk, making them stand at all perfect right angles to one another, with military precision. "But there's only one way to find out if I'm a man of my word."

"And that is?"

"Help me find her, and I'll prove it to you."

David shook his head immediately, every instinct inside him telling him that he should keep her hidden, just as he'd been doing, the past few months. But the truth was, this had dragged on too long. Mia was running out of options. Maybe this was the help she didn't know she needed, something that could finally bring her home to her family.

"What assurances do I have that you'll protect her? None?"

He backed away and threw up his hands. "Yep. If after I hear her side of the story, I still think she's guilty, I'll nail her ass to the wall. She will not be happy, once I get done with her, that's for sure. *But*," and here, he paused for effect and raised a finger. "If I have reason to believe she was the one who was screwed, like you and a little instinct within me seem to be shouting, then . . . I'll push with all the power I have to send her home, clear her name and scrub this whole thing from her record."

David paused, turning to face the window, overlooking the front of the Dallas Field Office parking lot, complete with American flag and large fountain. He thought about Mia, and what she would say, here. Mia liked to do things on her own. She used to be someone who didn't need the help. But in the past few months, she'd had to learn to accept help from whoever would give it to her.

And that was why he was almost positive, that if given this choice, she would probably take it.

David Hunter turned back and met his eyes.

I'm definitely going to be keeping an eye on you, and if this goes south, I'm *going to be the one nailing your ass to the wall.*

CHAPTER SIX

The Cedar Arms Luxury Trailer Village, near the Cedar Arms Reservoir in the town of Gun Springs City, wasn't exactly the lap of luxury.

When Mia looked out of the open window of Shilah's beaten Chevy pick-up, she hadn't expected much. She'd only been to Gun Springs City a few times in her life, and it was mostly a tourist destination, full of people enjoying the lovely reservoir. She didn't know it had rough neighborhoods like this.

But though the park was full of lovely, mature trees, the kind that kids love to climb and hang from, the trailers underneath looked like rotting corpses of their former selves. Most were coated in rust and dirt, like recently unearthed relics from an archaeological dig. They had small, dirty windows, and even the signs of hope and newness were sad—a beaten plastic slide, a sagging line of freshly-washed laundry, a half-full, deformed baby pool with a pattern of ducks in diapers, yellow pine needles floating on its surface. The ground was mostly dirt, but also covered with those pine needles, the road so heavily rutted that Mia bounced in the passenger seat.

"Home sweet home," Shilah said, pulling up in front of one of the trailers in the rear of the park. Though it was one of the bigger ones, it was also one of the older ones, too—a yellowing, rust-striped slab with brown shutters on the two inadequate windows in its front. Though some people had attempted to care for their homes with landscaping and flowers, Shilah's home was austere, the only décor on it a BEWARE OF DOG sign on the door.

"We don't have a dog," Shilah explained as she lumbered to the stairs. "So don't worry about that. Just keeps people from breaking in."

Mia nodded and followed.

As Shilah reached the top of the stairs, she pushed open the door and shouted, "Rocky, honey baby! I'm home! And I got a surprise for you!"

The place smelled overwhelmingly of bacon grease. It hit Mia like a knockout punch before she reached the top step. It opened up to a tiny kitchenette with a breakfast bar, all in harvest yellow. It was dark inside, with paneled walls and old paintings in embellished gold fames. There was a dark wood panel and flowered sofa beyond, with a patchwork of orange shag carpeting.

"Rocky!" Shilah shouted again, almost in Mia's ear. Then she sighed and marched into the living area.

Mia followed. A chubby teenage boy in a too-small black t-shirt sat on the floor, joystick in hand, glazed eyes focused on the television.

"Rocky!" Shilah said, waving a hand in front of his eyes. "It's Momma! I have a surprise for you! Come meet your momma's friend Mia. She's going to be staying with us for a few days."

He grunted but didn't look up. Mia had a wave and a hello at the ready, but she decided it'd be a waste.

"Rocky, baby. Want to give Momma a kiss?" she begged.

The boy grunted again.

Shilah gave her an apologetic shrug. "Sorry. He just got the new shoot 'em up game, and that's all he's been into for the past few days."

"It's all right," Mia said.

"If you come this way, I'll show you the extra room. You can stay there."

Shilah struggled to step over her son, and it was only when she took too long to move out of his line of vision that he shouted, "Mo-om! Come on! Get out of the way!" and lurched off to the side. His eyes finally tore away from the screen and he saw her.

She was about to wave, but the screen captured his interest once again, and he was lost. She quickly hopped over his legs and followed Shilah down a long hallway, past a small bathroom, to a room that was mostly filled with boxes.

"Here you go," Shilah said, flipping on the light to reveal more of it. In the middle of the boxes, Mia spotted a small bed. "It's not much. My uncle used to live here until he offed himself. So we just used it for storage."

"Oh, thanks."

She pulled open a closet door. There were more boxes inside. "You can put your clothes in—"

"Oh. I don't have any clothes, or anything, really . . ."

Shilah's eyes widened, and then she thunked her head. "Duh. Of course you don't. Well, you ain't my size, for sure, but I bet you were closer to Merry's. When we get done here, we can go over there and you can take what you need."

"You probably can't take anything from an active crime scene."

"Active?" She snorted, then laughed, long and loud. "Oh, girl. It's dead. Trust me. Last night I had to chase a couple of hoodlums away from it. They were trying to steal what little Merry had. No respect. And if you ask me, I don't think the police are coming back."

"Oh." Ordinarily, she'd have felt odd about taking a recently murdered woman's clothes, but she'd long since stopped caring about things like that. Plus, if she was going to be helping find the woman's murderer, she'd have to go through her things, anyway. "That would be great."

She stepped out into the hallway and her eyes caught on a framed photo on the wall. It was clearly a few decades old, but showed a pretty teenager, holding a bundled baby in her arms. The teenager had all the features of Shilah.

"That's me and Merry," she said with a sniff. "I raised her like she was my own, you know. Raised her from a little baby. My dad split right after she was born and my momma had to work. So it was always just the two of us, on our own."

Mia turned to face her, and though there were no tears, her eyes were glassy. Mia thought of her own older sister, Francine. They were close, too. Mia didn't cry easily, but if something had happened to Francine, Mia knew she'd be a mess. *How is this woman holding it together?*

She put a comforting hand on her shoulder as Shilah walked back toward the kitchen. There, they sat together at the kitchen counter, and Shilah poured them tea. "Now," she said as she set a chipped WORLD'S BEST MOM mug in front of Mia, "I don't got your expertise in solving crimes. In something like this, what would you do first—check out the scene of the crime?"

"I would want to do that, but not just yet," Mia said. "You really think the police are no longer investigating?"

She nodded. "Not only have they not been to Merry's trailer, but they don't come around Cedar Arms at all. Oh, they left their crime scene tape up, said they were investigating, but I think that's just talk. I haven't seen 'em here in two days."

"And you said the murder happened—"

"Three days ago. So they showed up, did their little dance, and left," she said, dropping into the chair across from Mia, which creaked under her weight. "Can't really say I blame them. A couple of officers were shot here, a few months ago. One was killed. You remember that?"

Mia shook her head. She'd been a little distracted by her own case while she was in prison. A nuclear bomb probably could've detonated in downtown Dallas, and she wouldn't have noticed. "They're pretty hostile toward law enforcement, then."

"They're pretty hostile toward *everyone*. The other murders that have happened around here. Gang related. Drug deals. That sort of thing."

That could be dangerous. This type was notoriously jittery when people came around, asking questions. She'd have to be tactful about it. "Still. I think it makes sense that you tell everyone I'm your cousin from out West," she said.

"Of course. You want to go over and see the place?"

"Not yet. What I would do first in these things would be to read up on the case file. But I can't do that, for obvious reasons. So why don't you tell me exactly what happened?" she said, wrapping her hands around the mug of tea. "When did you come in?"

"Rocky's on summer vacation, so I always bring him to Merry's place so she can watch him while I go to work at the warehouse. I got there at around eight-thirty, like I usually do, and she was lying there, in the doorway of her bedroom. Her whole midsection was covered in blood. I'll never forget it. She'd been stabbed," her voice wobbled.

"And then what happened?"

"I turned right around and shoved Rocky out so he wouldn't have to see his aunt like that. He's a sensitive boy. Then I called the police and they came in."

"Was anything different in the house, from what you remember?"

Shilah's lips twisted as she thought. "There was a gun next to her. I knew she kept one in the house but I didn't know where. So I think she might've heard a noise, went to investigate, and got stabbed by someone who came in before she could get a shot off. Because the screen was off the bedroom window. I saw it on the bed. Someone had pushed it in."

"And you explained that to the police?"

She rolled her eyes. “They didn’t care. They were more interested in the drug shit.”

“What was that?”

“There was a syringe on the coffee table and some traces of meth, or something. They took one look at that and chalked it up to a fight with her dealer.”

“Do you know who her dealer was?”

Shilah shook her head. “No. I stayed as far away from that sort of thing as possible.”

“Did they take her cell phone? With her contacts list?”

She nodded. “Oh. I guess it would probably be on there. Too bad.”

“Yeah, too bad,” she murmured, thinking as she took another sip of her tea. “Did you hear anything while they were investigating? Some theories you might have overheard?”

“Nah. They seemed really transfixed on the whole drug thing. I got the feeling they wanted to clear out of the place as soon as possible.”

Mia finished her tea. “All right. Well, when you’re ready, we can take a walk and you can show me around.”

Shilah took a gulp of her tea and struggled to stand. “I’m ready now. Let’s get this show on the road. Rocky! Going away for a minute, Sweetie, you hold the fort!”

No response.

Shilah balanced heavily on the railing as she labored to take the two steps to the ground. Mia stepped out, checking out the other nearby trailers. There was an old man in swimming trunks sitting in front of a small, bullet trailer, his feet in a baby pool, his doughy skin covered by snow white hair and a sheen of sweat. He watched them carefully as they walked past.

Mia smiled. “Nice day, isn’t it?”

He simple scowled at her.

Shilah took her arm. “Don’t mind old Gruver. He’s a grump. He’s out there twenty-four seven, giving people nasty looks.”

Mia didn’t say anything, but it immediately made her curious. Old, nosy neighbors were often the best witnesses. Had old Gruver seen something?

Shilah walked her down the narrow road. “So, that’s Gruver’s old trailer. He’s been here since this place opened, back in the seventies. And over there is Marty—I don’t see much of her because she has like, twelve kids under the age of six. I don’t know how she does it, or how she did it, if you ask me. They all got different daddies. Sometimes I think half of them ain't even hers, but who am I to judge?" She pointed out another trailer, pale pink, with flowers outside. "That's a kid named Roan—he's seventeen. And his mom. They're quiet. Good folk."

Mia nodded, making mental notes of all the names, so that she could try to find a way to talk to them. As they walked down the path, they passed a few more people. Shilah didn't wave at any of them. Mia could feel their gazes, boring into her back.

"Wow, everyone here is so . . . friendly," Mia said, watching a little girl playing with a hula hoop who couldn't have been more than five, giving them the same stink-eye.

"I told you," Shilah said, motioning to a large, one-story structure with a front porch set up with a few picnic tables. "Everyone here keeps to themselves. Over here is the local area store and restaurant, if you want something to eat. I wouldn't try to get all fancy, I got food poisoning there once, from the chicken patty sandwich."

"Noted."

Shilah shuffled on, stopping at a metal slide, a set of primitive metal monkey bars, a weed-filled sandbox, and a tree with a tire swing. "Our playground."

There were no kids on it, even though it was the middle of day. Too hot, likely. "Looks nice."

Shilah put her hands on her hips, took a deep breath, and motioned with her double-chin to a pink trailer that was in danger of being swallowed by the many weeds surrounding it. "That one was Merry's," she said solemnly. "Are you ready?"

Mia looked over at it, and let out the breath she'd been holding. From the look on Shilah's face, she wasn't ready in the least. "Yes. Lead the way."

But as they were about to take a step in that direction, the sound of screaming sirens greeted them.

Heart in her throat, Mia froze.

CHAPTER SEVEN

Mia looked around for a place to hide, but Shilah stood there, unconcerned. She was just about to retreat when the police cars arrived in a cloud of dust. Mia stopped, knowing it would only look more suspicious if she ran.

The police officers jumped out and ran to a trailer down the road, banging on the flimsy door. "Open up!" A moment later, they broke down the door and pulled out a man in an undershirt, flinging him on the ground and cuffing him.

Mia stared, half-relieved, half-horrified that no one seemed to care. The girl with the hula hoop kept right on hula-hooping, as if this was an everyday occurrence.

When they shoved their culprit into the back of the police car and drove away, Mia let out a sigh of relief and gradually shifted her mind back to the task at hand. The murder.

She waited for Shilah to lead the way to the murder scene. But the woman's feet were planted, and she was looking up at the trailer.

"It was my aunt's, but when she died, Merry had a boyfriend and they was looking for a place, so rather than sell it I let them have it." Shilah laughed and slapped her fleshy side. "You ever have to clean a house to get it sold? Not fun. I didn't want to have to deal with it so I was glad when they came in. I charged them half the rent of the place they were going to lease. So it was win-win."

She was clearly procrastinating. It was only when Shilah spoke that Mia noticed the small strip of crime scene tape that must've gone across the door, now waving in the breeze like a flag. It was definitely inadequate. "Did you clean up the scene yet?"

She shook her head. "Me? I ain't been back there since I found her. And this kind of cleaning is worse than cleaning a house to sell. They told me I could hire someone and it'd be covered by my insurance, but I don't trust that."

Of course, that made sense. If they were telling her to bring in the bioremediation specialists to do the clean-up, that meant they were done and moving on. "You should probably hire someone. They have people who specialize in things like this. It's not exactly a pleasant task to clean it yourself, you know. And it could be dangerous."

Shilah nodded. "I know."

"And if you want to sell it, now, you can probably find a company that will come in to sanitize the whole place," Mia explained. "Make it good as new for the new buyers. You wouldn't have to lift a finger."

"I suppose," she said with a sigh. Still, she didn't move, her eyes locked on the target.

"Shilah?" Mia said gently.

"Huh?"

"Let's go." She tugged on the sleeve of her t-shirt. "Come on. I'll go in first, if you want."

Taking a deep breath, she lumbered over and opened the door. This time, she stepped aside and let Mia take the lead.

The trailer was much lighter, and in Mia's opinion, nicer than the one Shilah was living in. She noticed the couch, a jacket or shirt casually draped over its arm, and the old coffee table, a glass of half-consumed soda on it. It looked as if whoever lived there had just stepped out and would be back at any moment.

But then Mia heard the buzzing. Flies.

She turned her head and craned her neck, looking down the hallway, and that was when she saw it.

As far as crime scenes went, this one was rather tame. She'd been to scenes that were virtual horror shows, with blood sprayed over walls and ceilings, like some child's finger painting. But the only thing that was striking about this one was a small, smeared puddle of brownish dried blood on the parquet floor, right at the entrance to the last room in the hallway.

As she came closer to it, the flies were having a field day on it, taking off and then landing again on the dried surface. She waved her hand in front of her face as she came closer. There was a handprint in blood on the door jamb, small, probably belonging to the victim. No doubt, the police had photographed and catalogued all of this.

She turned on a light in the hallway to get a better look at where the body had lain, then scanned the area. She saw the screen from the window, lying on top of the unmade bed, and the open window, large enough for another person to climb through. Stepping over the blood stain, she went to the window and looked for any signs from the perpetrator. There was a little dirt on the window ledge, and as she stuck her head out, she noticed some footprints below the door. They were big, probably male.

This was nothing revolutionary. All these things, the police had probably noted. The only difference was, she was willing to look into it.

When she turned around and began to head toward the front door, she saw Shilah standing there, facing away, half bent over a table, breathing hard. She looked like she was having a heart attack.

"Is everything okay?" Mia asked.

Shilah nodded, but refused to turn. "Oh, just fine," she said breezily.

Mia inched around her and saw that her face was red. She was deliberately trying to avoid looking down that hallway. Mia grabbed her arm and helped her out of the trailer. She stood in the doorway, while Shilah stood on the ground in front of her, taking deep breaths until the panic attack passed. "You all right?"

Shilah nodded. "Fine. Whew. Just got a little woozy. It was stuffy in there, no?"

"Yeah, it was."

"Did you notice anything?"

Mia shrugged. "Well, it's a little hard to tell without the body. But what I can say is that you're right, it does look like she was surprised and that whoever it was came in through the bedroom window. Looks like she heard a noise and was hoping to defend herself with the gun. You didn't notice anything stolen?"

Shilah said, "Merry didn't have nothing to steal. I stopped charging her rent when Dirk—that was her boyfriend— moved out because she started sitting for Rocky. But that was a year ago. Anything she had, I got the feeling it went to drugs, because she was always asking me for money for gas, or stopping by my place to eat breakfast. And—she took the money I kept in my cookie jar, for emergencies."

"I see. The place doesn't look like it's been ransacked, which means we can rule out theft as a motive. Seems to me that it's likely personal. Can you give me a list of Merry's friends and acquaintances?"

Shilah shook her head. "You know I was in prison for a while, and when I got out, I was just getting back on my feet. Didn't really have much time to settle into things, so I don't know . . ."

"What about this Dirk guy?"

“I heard he moved to Kentucky. Had a job there. She didn’t want to go. That’s why they broke things off.”

Mia gnawed on her lip, thinking, as she scanned the area. From here, there were three trailers in view. She was looking at the back-side of them, since Merry’s was set back farther than all of them. “What about these trailers? Did she know the neighbors here? Do you?”

Shilah stroked her jaw. “Yeah . . . that one’s empty, as far as I know.” She pointed at the closest trailer. The windows were blocked off and it looked like the ceiling had caved in. “Probably a drug or make-out den for some kids, like the ones I saw trying to break in before. That one over there is Old Miss Mussman, who’s older than the hills. Merry and I took turns doing errands for her. She’s not bad.” She pointed to another one, practically invisible among the trees. “And that one is Long Face.”

“Long Face?”

She nodded. “I don’t know his name. Guy has a crazy long face. Like I swear, goes on for miles. Long body, too. Tall drink of water, that one is. He doesn’t say anything to no one. Just stands outside and stares, sometimes. Most of the time, he’s inside. You can tell because you can see the glow of the television from his window.” She shuddered. “He is a creep.”

She looked around, noting how remote the trailer was. The way it was situated, no other trailer faced it. So whoever had done it could’ve easily gotten in, without anyone noticing. “Interesting. How long have they been here?”

“Mussman, since the dawn of time, probably. But she walks with a walker. So I don’t see her climbing in windows.”

Mia nodded.

“Long Face, though . . . I don’t know. Five years? I always thought there was something wrong with him. The way he leers at me. You think he could’ve done it?”

She shook her head. “Not necessarily. If he’s been here that long, it would be odd for him to just snap one day and decide to kill, if they never had a relationship before, that you know of?”

“I don’t know of one,” Shilah admitted. “But like I said, I’ve been busy.”

Mia turned and took one last look around the place. As she did, she noticed something attached to the refrigerator in the kitchen. It was one of those wipe-off boards that people used to record things they needed. On it, it mostly scrubbed away and faded, it seemed to say, "Cal ick."

"Who's Ick?" she asked.

Shilah's eyes narrowed. "Ick?"

"Yeah. It's on her note board. I-C-K. Ick. Probably part of another name. Rick? Dick?"

Shilah shook her head slowly. "I don't know. Doesn't ring a bell. Sorry."

"It's all right," she said, stepping out of the trailer and closing the door behind her.

"Oh," Shilah said. "Didn't you want to go through the closet and find some of Merry's clothes to wear?"

"Later," Mia said, heading toward the other trailers. She would have to do that, eventually, but now she had the scent of something, and she didn't want to lose it. "Right now, I'm going to be nosy and ask a few questions."

CHAPTER EIGHT

When Shilah left to go back to check on Rocky, Mia decided that her best chance of piecing together who had killed Merry would be with the old woman. In her experience, the elderly often saw crimes being committed, not just because they had more time on their hands and a tendency to be nosier, but because they often quietly sat back, unnoticed, letting things happen. It wasn't just that criminals didn't see them as a threat—sometimes, they didn't see them at all.

But as she navigated over to the small trailer tucked into the corner of the park, she could've sworn someone was watching her.

Looking over her shoulder, toward Long Face's trailer, she could've sworn she saw the blinds in one window dip slightly. It might've just been her imagination, but the silence of the morning was eerie, even though birds were chirping overhead. It was like the whole place was holding its breath, waiting for something terrible to happen.

Old Miss Mussman's trailer bore the signs of someone trying to take care of it and give it curb appeal—but that someone had abandoned those projects, long ago. The windows had pretty, storybook shutters with hearts carved in the center, but they needed painting. There were flower boxes under the windows, but they were overgrown with weeds, only the occasional wild daisy poking out from the scraggle of vegetation. There was a welcome mat on the ground outside on the tiny landing in front of the front door, but it was so worn, the words WELCOME FRIENDS were faded almost to nothing.

Mia pressed the doorbell once. Then, thinking the old lady might be hard of hearing, she pressed it again. *She's in there,* Shilah had told her, before she set out. *Doesn't go anywhere. You might just need to rattle the door a little to get her to respond.*

She grabbed the door handle and rattled it, just as Shilah had said.

"Come in!" a voice croaked.

Mia opened the door, but it got caught on a plush seafoam green carpet, so she had to shove it hard in order to create a space large enough for her to step through. The living area was full of roses—wallpaper of roses on trellises, rose upholstered furniture, lampshades imprinted with them. It even smelled like them, not like actual roses, but like the air-freshener. There were bouquets of blatantly fake ones in a rainbow of colors, all over the room.

Miss Mussman sat kicked back in a lounge chair, slippered feet up. She was wearing a pink housecoat that bared her matchstick-like, liver-spotted legs, and her hair had once been dyed a startling orange, but now, it was half-smoky, wispy gray at the roots. She was facing Mia, but there was an old console television set between them. Mia could hear the strains of a game show announcer's voice, talking about "fabulous prizes."

"Oh, I thought you were Shilah," she said with disappointment.

"No, I'm actually Shilah's cousin," Mia said, remembering the lie. "I'm staying with her a few days."

"She was supposed to come and give me my prescription," the woman said, not taking her eyes off the television. "I'm almost out of my heart pill."

This was actually a good thing. She could work with it, so that she didn't come off as nosy law enforcement. "Oh, well, she's busy. She told me to come over and get it."

Her watery blue eyes, rimmed with deep lines, finally fell on Mia. "You said you're her cousin?" She said it like she didn't believe it.

Mia nodded.

"She never mentioned a cousin before."

Mia smiled. "Well, that's good ol' Shilah. Always forgetting about me," she said with a shrug. "I'm from out west. Just came to help out, you know, because of her tragedy?"

The woman pressed her thin lips together. "I do. Poor young girl." She motioned behind her, to the kitchen. "Prescription's on the counter, and I have a few items to pick up at the store."

Mia crossed the living area, her feet sinking into the heavily padded carpet, and found the list and the prescription. She'd give them to Shilah to take care of when she got back, since it wasn't exactly possible for her to go to the store right now.

What she wanted to do was somehow sway things more to the topic of the murdered girl. She turned. "It was a real shock for Shilah, to hear that about her sister."

"Oh, yes. How is she doing?"

"Obviously, not so well. Trying to get things together."

The woman nodded and motioned to an empty plate, with the remains of what looked like blueberries, on a folding table, beside the recliner. It soon became obvious to her that the old woman wanted her to do something with it. So Shilah and Merry, when they came here, tidied up, too. Mia took it and brought it to the sink. As she washed it and dried it, she said, "Did you know Merry well?"

"Of course. She came here every other day and checked up on me. Sometimes we'd play backgammon. We were friends. Do you play?"

Mia slipped the dish into the empty spot on the holder and turned to find the woman opening a case that had a backgammon board in it and setting up the various pieces.

"Uh, I haven't in a while. But sure," she said, taking a nearby chair and moving it up to the table. "As long as your prescription can wait?"

"It can. This old ticker isn't about to give up yet," she said, shaking the dice in the container. "Merry never beat me yet."

I guess she'll never beat you, now, Mia thought, as she watched the woman excitedly throw the dice and move her pieces. "It's nice that you were friends. Looking out for each other. Sure was a surprise that she was killed. I was shocked when I heard it."

She snorted and looked up at Mia. "You were? I sure wasn't."

Mia took the container with the dice for her turn and paused. "What do you mean by that?"

"This is a bad neighborhood, and she was involved in bad things."

"Like?"

The old woman motioned for her to move on with her turn. Mia had almost forgotten they were playing. She threw the dice and tried to remember the strategy, but in the end, just moved the first two pieces she got her hands on the correct number of spots, because she was so interested in what the woman was saying. "Men. All sorts of bad men coming over there. I think they dealt drugs. I felt terrible for that little boy when he lived with her. But Shilah came back and took him off her hands. After that, the men kept coming, and she got worse. Stopped coming to see me."

Mia handed the dice back to the woman, who threw them at once and started to move. "Do you know who they were?"

She woman tapped her fingers on her chin, her eyes fastened on the board as she tried to figure out her move. "Yes, that one guy, with no hair. Know him well. Name of Mike."

"Mike?"

"Yep. He's the one who did her in. Sure about that."

Mia gazed at her in surprise. "He was?"

"Oh, yes. I saw him, out the back window of my bedroom, making a bloody ruckus, knocking on her door while I was trying to sleep. I'm hard of hearing and I could hear it, plain as day. Guy was demanding money. The next morning, she turned up dead." Now, even the old woman had temporarily forgotten about the game. She shuddered. "I told her. I told her that moth was going to get her."

"Moth?" Mia asked in confusion. "Oh, you mean the meth?"

"Right. I told her that dealer was no good. That Mike."

"Do you know anything about him? Like where he lives . . . does he live in this neighborhood? Do you know what kind of car he drives?"

She narrowed her eyes. "Why are you asking? You and Shilah think you're going to dole out some justice? I told the police to get off my porch, and I'll tell you the same if you think you're going to get that guy. You don't get it. It's not just him. He's part of a big network. You give it to him, two more spring up in their place, and they don't look kindly on tattle-tales. They'll come after you, and they'll come after me if we interfere. So I'm not telling no one, nothing. You tell the police what I saw and they ask me, I'll deny the whole thing. I just want to stay out of it."

Mia nodded. "I understand. I just think it would bring Shilah peace to know who the killer was."

The woman laughed bitterly as she moved her piece. "Ain't no peace in this neighborhood. The only peace you get is if you keep to yourself, as much as you can."

Mia took the dice, shaking them. It clearly was going to do no good asking more about this Mike character. She wasn't going to tell her. Her best bet was to see if there was anyone else in the neighborhood who might know him, too. "So other than Shilah and Merry, what about the rest of the people who live around here?"

"They all stay to themselves, like they should. I don't know any of them. Not like when I was young and we all knew each other, said hello in passing. Now, you say hello to the wrong person and you get your block knocked off, a bullet in your head for your troubles." She shook her head as Mia moved her first piece into the last space. "I'm careful."

"What about Long Face?"

Miss Mussman looked up. "Who?"

Mia pointed. "Trailer over there. Next to yours?"

"Oh. Him. He's quiet. Shilah thinks he's a creep but I don't know enough. Never bothered me." She shook the dice in the container. "And before you go asking, the trailer on the other side is empty. So no one there saw nothing. But like I said, if you dig too deep, you're going to get your nose cut off, girl . . .cousin. What's your name again?"

"Sue," she said, using the name she'd used in the past.

"Right. Sue. If I were you, I'd bury the dead and drop it. That's all." She looked down and moved her pieces. "Ha! A twelve. Would you look at that. I win again."

"That's great," Mia said, standing up and moving the chair back. "If there's nothing else you need, I'd better get over to the store and pick these things up."

Miss Mussman shook her head. "You go on. And give Shilah my best."

"I will."

She stepped outside and walked down the steps, looking in both directions, trying to decide whether to tackle Long Face, now, if he would even talk to her.

Deciding it would take less time, she turned toward the abandoned trailer. As she got closer, she saw that it was definitely abandoned, the windows boarded up and the screen door hanging ajar, though a large plank of plywood had been placed over the opening. Graffiti of various colors covered it, and the outside was dented, as if a massive fist had punched it.

She stared at some of the symbols painted on the side of the trailer. She'd seen them before, while patrolling some of the worst neighborhoods in Dallas. They were gang symbols.

As she moved closer, she realized the plank of wood over the door had been pushed back slightly, allowing just enough room for a body to slip through.

Curious, she moved closer, peering into the darkness, and as her eyes adjusted, she noticed two eyes, staring straight back at her.

CHAPTER NINE

Mia jumped back as a voice called, “Who the hell are you?”

It sounded almost like a child’s, but the tone was more adult. There was a shuffling inside as someone said, “Come on, Cut, let’s blow this joint.”

As she watched, three boys, no more than thirteen or fourteen, in jeans and t-shirts, scrambled out of the opening. They raced past her, on the way toward the front of the trailer park. She could smell the pot on them.

“Wait. Guys!” she called after them.

They didn’t even pause. They kept running, scattering and disappearing among the bushes that lined the street.

It probably wasn’t worth it to run after them. They looked young, but they probably had siblings who were gangbangers, so they knew the rules. Likely, they were all like Miss Mussman, not willing to say anything for fear of getting killed by the gangs that lorded over this place.

Pushing aside the plank of wood, she hoisted herself into the abandoned trailer.

Now, it was empty, and it looked like the place had been not only ransacked, but gutted. Everything that hadn’t been nailed down was gone now, and the walls were all covered with graffiti. Not only did heavy smoke from a recently toked joint fill the air, but there were needles and other drug paraphernalia, as well as dozens of beer cans, littering the ground. Rags were set up as cushions, since the floor was missing its carpet. Mia kicked through them, then went to one of the boarded windows in the back of the trailer that would’ve looked out upon Merry’s home. It was still intact.

If someone was here when the murder occurred, they would likely have seen nothing.

As she spun, she saw it—a tiny bag full of weed. She picked it up, inspecting it. It would’ve been nice if it had the name of the supplier on it, but suppliers weren’t that stupid. Making sure the zip lock on it was fastened, she tucked it in her pocket.

Slipping out, she marched across the rutted dirt, toward Long Face's home. The blinds were all drawn, and there was an old Cadillac, parked in front of the door.

She climbed the steps, took a deep breath, and knocked on the door.

A man answered right away, and yes, he had a rather long face, but Mia had not been expecting anything else she saw. Yes, he was tall, but not eight-feet-tall, like she was expecting from Shilah's description. He was older, with dark, close-cropped hair and a red cardigan sweater that made him look a bit like Mr. Rogers. His eyes seemed rather kind, and his voice, as he said, "Yes?" was quiet and kind, as well.

It was so off-putting that she realized she hadn't yet come up with a cover story for knocking on his door. "Uh, hello," she fumbled, her mind churning with ideas. "I'm here, visiting my cousin, Shilah . . . do you know her?"

He removed his wire-rimmed glasses and shook his head. "I'm sorry. I'm not interested."

He went to close the door. "But—" she blurted, reaching her hand out to stop him.

He frowned at her, then opened the door wider, so she could see a bit more into the trailer. A screen glowed in the corner of the living area. It wasn't a television she saw, like Shilah had said, but a large, modern desktop computer monitor. It looked like he was in the middle of writing something.

"Oh, I'm sorry, I just came to—"

"Are you selling something?" He was losing patience. "Because—"

She blurted, "No, I just—my cousin, Merry, over there, was murdered a few days ago."

He stopped and nodded, his voice becoming kind again. "Ah. Yes. I know of that. I saw the police come. That's terrible."

"The family's really beside themselves because they don't know who did it. I was wondering if you knew anything?"

He shook his head. "Unfortunately, I keep to myself. I'm working on my latest project and I'm afraid it takes all my time, so I haven't had much time to get to know people. Plus, I'm not interested in anything that goes on out there."

"Your latest . . . project?"

He nodded. "I'm an author."

"Oh, really? Have you written anything I might have read?"

He looked over her. "Doubtful. I write science fiction novels. Is that an interest of yours?"

"No, can't say it is," she admitted.

He sighed. "You're not alone."

"So, you didn't hear anything on the night she was murdered? Because I was looking at your house, and your window on this side looks right out onto the front of her trailer. And it looks like someone climbed through her bedroom window, which you'd have a perfect view of."

He shook his head. "Sorry. I was busy with my book."

"Did you happen to hear of a fight that might've taken place that night? Someone knocking, demanding drug money?"

He blinked. "Wait. That was the night she was killed?"

Mia nodded. "You remember it?"

"I do," he said, shaking his head. "He was making enough noise to wake the dead. He started to scream at whoever lived there, and I heard the woman open the door and scream back. She must've let him in, because when I looked out, the door was open and I think he was inside."

"Did you hear anything they might have said?"

"Yes, well, she told him to go away, but he said he wouldn't leave without his money," he said, stroking his chin. "I suppose it was about drugs. I hear they're pretty prevalent around here. What I assumed was that she might've taken drugs from him that weren't strictly hers, and he expected payment."

Mia nodded. "Can you tell me about the man?"

"He had a shaved head. And I saw tattoos. Looked like a thug," he said with a shrug. "I'd seen him around here before, and—"

He paused, then snapped his fingers.

"Mick. His name was Mick."

Mick. So not Mike. That made sense. It was the name written on Merry's refrigerator, the person she had to call. "Do you know where he came from? What kind of car he was driving?"

"He had a motorcycle. A big one. I'm not familiar with types, though. Just a big cycle. I don't know where he came from."

"Did you happen to see him leave?"

"I didn't, but I heard him. A few minutes later. That motorcycle was so loud, I can't imagine anyone in the neighborhood wouldn't hear him."

That was a good point. Based on the crime scene, he hadn't entered through the front door. So if he was the killer, he'd likely gone away on his cycle, then come back, only to enter through the bedroom window. "Did you see or hear anything after that? Anyone at all?"

"No. Unfortunately, I was busy with my writing after that. I don't recall anything. I had assumed he got what he wanted, but maybe he didn't. Maybe he was so angry at her, he came back and got his revenge." He stepped back, and his jaw set, shortening his long face somewhat. "Now, if you'll excuse me, I do need to get back to my book."

"Yes, of course."

"Again, sorry about your cousin, it's a very sad thing," he said, closing the door on her.

It occurred to her as she stood there, how people's perceptions could be so wildly different. Here, Shilah had thought Long Face was some crazy misanthrope, but really, he came across as quite normal, just a quiet man looking for solitude. Thinking about the conversation, she wondered where to go next. As she spun to head down the stairs, she noticed someone moving by the abandoned trailer.

Craning her neck, she made out the person's features—the black t-shirt and the faded jeans, and the scraggly long hair, tucked under a trucker's cap.

It was one of the boys, she'd seen earlier. He was pushing back the plywood, peering into the trailer, looking for something.

Mia had a good idea of what he was missing.

She crept up behind him and crossed her arms. "Looking for something?"

He spun on her and gasped like a pearl-clutching old lady in front of a sinner. "What are you—who are you?"

She pulled out his bag of weed and dangled it in front of him. "Why don't you let me ask the questions?"

He swiped for it, but she easily pulled it away from his reach and wagged a finger at him.

"I'll give this to you. But not until you answer my questions."

"Hell no." He reached into his pocket and pulled out a switchblade, which he sprung open. "How about I just cut you instead?"

She rolled her eyes and held out her hands to appease him. Why did kids today feel like they needed to blow up every situation into a crisis? "You don't want to do that. Come on, just--"

He lunged suddenly, jabbing the blade in her direction, but she easily sidestepped it and grabbed a hold of his wrist, forcing him to drop it. He was only a kid, so she didn't throw all of her weight at him as she spun him around, shoving him face-first against the side of the trailer. "Hey, I told you not to do that," she said sweetly as he moaned and broke out in tears.

"Leave me alone! Don't hurt me! Don't—" he whined.

She looked around, hoping no one saw this. If she wanted to keep a low profile, this probably wasn't the way to do it. "Shh. Kid, I'm not going to hurt you. I just have one question for you, and then you can go. Okay?"

He nodded, sniffling, snot running from the end of his nose. "Okay."

"Who's your provider?"

He sobbed, his breaths coming in short bursts. "I don't know! I don't do drugs. I don't—"

"Don't give me that B.S. I know you were coming back to get your weed. You get it from a guy named Mick, right?"

He sniffled, then nodded, almost imperceptibly.

"Where do you go to get it? Do you know where he lives?" she said, still holding tight to his arm as she pressed it behind his back.

"W-why?"

"Maybe I want to get some, too."

"Y-you don't look like the type. You look like a cop," he said.

Funny. Here she was in dirty jeans, a ponytail, unwashed for days, and she still managed to come off as law enforcement. She said, "Are you going to tell me, or not? I won't tell anyone where I got the information. I just need to know."

"It's a cabin. In the woods. About a mile up Pike Street. Maybe a little more. It has a red metal roof."

"Where on Pike Street?"

"I don't . . . all I know is, at the main road, we went left. It's pretty hidden. I was pretty wasted the last time we went, so I don't know any more."

She slowly let him go, then stepped back, grabbing his knife and the bag of weed from the ground. She held it up for him. When he went to take it, she said, "You know, I know there is all this talk about weed being *fine,* but when I was growing up, scientists said it killed brain cells. The weed hasn't changed, but something has. You understand what I mean?"

He stared at her blankly.

Finally, she just tossed it at him, closed the knife, and handed it over to him. "Get out of here."

He took his belongings and ran off. She sighed.

Then she turned back to go to Shilah's trailer. She had to make sure to get Miss Mussman's prescription and shopping list to her friend, so that she could set off on her own adventure—checking out this cabin in the woods.

CHAPTER TEN

The man walked down the aisles full of rotting trailers in the middle of the day, cursing the place.

It was like Grand Central Station around here, people so busy doing anything and everything. Checking each other out. Shooting their veins full of poison. Making bets on the next game on television. Wasting away in lounge chairs and chatting up a storm about how they never had enough money to afford anything.

They were doing everything they could . . . but work.

In the *middle of the day.*

Far be it for any of them to—oh, possibly—get a job. That was too much for any of these deadbeats to handle.

He knew it well. And he also knew that not a single one of the residents had the brain power to know what had happened in the back of that trailer park, a few nights ago. Dumb, dumb, dumb . . . or high as kite. Every last one of them.

"Hey, want to play catch?" A little kid came up to him, holding a football.

He smiled at the kid, as he sucked on his cigarette. *Shouldn't these little pissants be in school?* That was one thing these parents loved—school, the chance to let someone else babysit their kids for eight hours of the day.

Then he remembered summer vacation. His summer vacations had always bled into the school year because it was nothing but misery, every day, from morning 'til night.

Some kids have all the luck.

"Sure," he said, backing up. "Toss it here."

The kid threw it like a rocket, right into his hand. He tossed it back, impressed.

"You got a good arm, kid." *Too bad in this slum, you're never gonna get anywhere.*

He tossed the ball back and forth with the kid, all the while looking at the other people in the park. Places like this were all the same. Bunch of teenage hooligans hanging out, talking about where to score drugs.

The girls in the group, showing too much skin, would probably be pregnant by sixteen. All the result of parents who didn't give a shit and kept passing down the indifference from generation to generation.

It had to stop somewhere.

As far as he was concerned, it *needed* to stop.

As he tossed the ball to the kid, a fat woman with tattoos up and down her cellulite-rippled legs called to him from where she was sunning herself on a picnic bench. "Leo! Get inside and get me a lemonade."

The kid missed the ball. He froze, then said, "Okay, Momma!" He rushed to the door, then stopped, remembering him. "Sorry, I got to go."

The man nodded, and the kid ran off, slamming the door behind him. When he did, the man looked at the fat mother, tilting her face to the sun like she was some kind of goddess in her black sunglasses.

Disgusting pig.

That's what all these people were. They shouldn't have been allowed to breed.

He smiled as he walked along, thinking about how the police had been so spooked by the riff-raff, they'd only done a quick sweep of the place. They had the wrong idea, thinking she was killed as part of the raging drug war. If they'd looked into it even just a little more, they might've seen the similarities between the young woman's death and the murder of the old lady, in the spring. It was practically spoon-fed to them. He hadn't even tried to hide it.

But the police didn't care. No one cared. These people were expendable. He had to agree with the police on that point.

If these people didn't give a shit about anyone or anything, why should anyone give a shit about them?

The thought made him giddy. It meant that he could have a little more fun. He had a list of names, of people who were just asking for it. They were just waiting for him.

And no one would be there to stop him.

All he had to do was step in, and take his revenge. He could barely wait.

CHAPTER ELEVEN

Mia sat in the front passenger's seat of Shilah's pick-up, bouncing along the rutted road. The prescription and list sat in the cup holder, between them. She held her hands together to keep them from shaking. Though she never had minded working alone, Mia wished she had the help of her sidearm, or her partner, or *something* to confront this drug dealer. This felt a little like going into battle without any armor.

Just going to talk to him. Just going to pretend to be a customer. It'll be fine, she told herself as they bumped along the rutted road, to front of the trailer park. As Shilah pulled out onto Pike Avenue, she said, "This way?"

"That's what he said."

She drove along, squinting at the trees. "I know there are some houses up this way, but they're far from the road. You said a red roof?"

"Yep."

Shilah drove slowly, so they wouldn't miss it. "Are you sure you don't want me to—"

"No, if you come, you'll break my cover. Besides, I can handle it," she said, pointing to the list. "And Miss Mussman needs her heart pill."

"But when you're done—"

"It's not far. The kid said only about a mile. So I'll walk back."

Shilah gnawed on her cheek. "I still think this could be risky."

"The police won't get involved, right? Somebody has to do it," she said with a shrug. "Besides, you're being nice, offering me a place to stay. It'll be like earning my keep."

"If you wanted to do that, you could just sit for Rocky while I'm at work," she mumbled.

"Trust me. That's probably more dangerous than this. I've never raised boys before," she said with a smile, doing her best to conceal her nervousness as she looked out the window. "Stop!"

Shilah slammed on the brakes and Mia pointed.

Through the heavy greenery, there was a small flash of red. A rusty mailbox, was on an old post, tilted toward the road, with the faded words *111 Pike Avenue* written on the side. A narrow driveway, just two tire ruts, headed into a canopy of dark trees.

"I think this is my stop." She pulled the handle and slid out. "I'll be back soon."

"Good luck," Shilah said, eyebrows knitted with worry.

Mia slammed the door and Shilah drove on.

She turned toward the house, trying to see it among the trees. The driveway stretched about a quarter mile, curving slightly, and she followed it up, seeing and hearing no one. When the cover of trees separated and she found the clearing, she hung back, scanning the area and sniffing the air. There was a strange smell in it, harsh and acrid, like ammonia.

She didn't have to be a DEA agent to know what a meth lab smelled like.

The cabin was an A-frame, made of dark wood in desperate need of staining. There was a small patio in the front, devoid of any patio furniture. Trees surrounding the home towered over it, which must've made it dark inside, because even though it was mid-day, she could clearly see a light, shining in one of the front windows.

There was also a motorcycle and a beaten, old-model Ford Bronco, parked out front.

Someone was definitely home.

She took a step, only a single step, toward the house, when she heard a familiar sound. It was a bang, and almost instantaneously, she heard the leaves rustle to her right, and something embedding itself in a tree trunk.

Gunfire.

She threw herself to the ground, pain screaming at her knees as a voice called, "Get the hell out of here."

He fired again, this one going far wide. He was intentionally missing.

She squinted, looking for a body to go along with that voice, but she saw nothing. She heard another gunshot and ducked her head. Scanning the area, she saw a ravine, and dove for it.

The door of the cabin opened and a man appeared there. He couldn't have been more than his late twenties. His head was mostly bald, except for a shock of dark hair, right at the front, and he had barbed-wire tattoos on his neck, stretching up to both of his temples.

He was wearing a baseball shirt and jeans, holding a pistol, eyes darting across the trees.

He marched toward her, scanning the trees for her.

The second he passed by, she dove on his back, quickly grabbing the gun. He threw his arms back, trying to lose her, and dove for the gun, but she got there first, grabbing it and throwing an arm around his neck.

"Get off me!" he cried. "What the hell?"

CHAPTER TWELVE

"Stop!" Mia shouted as the man flailed, trying to get away. She grabbed his gun and pointed it toward him. "Stop fighting me."

"Let go of me. Do you not understand English? This is private property and you need to get the hell out."

"Are you Mick?" she cried, disbelieving. Paranoid, much? Is this the way he did business with all of his customers? How did he make any sales if all he did was shoot at anyone who came down the driveway?

A pause. "Who's asking?"

"A customer . . . well, actually, a potential customer."

"I don't sell to anyone unless I know them. Who sent you?"

She thought fast, remembering what those kids in the abandoned trailer had said. "Cut."

"Cut?" He looked confused.

She let go of him, still holding his gun. "I live in Cedar Arms. He's a kid. We call him Cut. He said you sold him and his friends some weed."

To her relief, he nodded. "Oh, yeah. Mr. Cutlass. I do remember those kids. What are you, their mother?"

She shrugged. "I'm a friend of their mother. I wanted to know . . . do you just sell pot?"

He motioned to his gun. "Give that back to me, and we'll talk."

She grabbed it by the barrel and gave him the handle. He took it, shoving it into the front of his jeans.

"All right, now, let's talk business." He clapped his hands together.

"Good. Do you have anything stronger?"

A smile appeared on his face, which grew to a laugh. "Do I have anything stronger? Seriously?" He looked around. "I *might*, but then again, I don't sell out of my house. It's too dangerous."

"The boys knew where to find you," Mia pointed out. "And they're not exactly expert trackers."

He let out a long sigh. "Yeah. Because boys like to play in the woods and they found me. But it's too dangerous if too many people know where to find me. You understand? So if we do business, you don't tell anyone, or I'll cut that tongue out of your pretty little mouth."

She shrugged. "Fine, fine. I'm not going to tell anyone. Meth. Do you have it? I smell it."

He put a finger to his lips. "Jesus. Quiet. I might be out in the middle of the woods, but there are people all over who'd love the chance to bust this operation. That's why I've got the cameras." He pointed to one, its lens aimed directly at her. Then he swung around to leave. "Get out of here and you won't get yourself killed."

In desperation, she called, "Whatever you charge, I'll pay double."

It was a lie, and she regretted it the second it came out of her mouth, because she had no money.

But it worked, nonetheless. He stopped and turned. "All right. Come in before I change my mind."

She walked across the gravel driveway, climbed the three steps to the empty deck, and crossed it. Even before she went in the sliding glass door, she saw that this wasn't an ordinary vacation cabin.

The acrid smell made her eyes water, the moment she stepped inside. There was no furniture, except for a beaten sofa in the corner. The place had been cleared out expressly for the purpose of cooking up the drug, with large vats of material, burners, plastic jars and other things one would be more likely to find in a lab than in a rustic cabin.

He presented it to her proudly, like a father presenting his only son. "Yeah, I've been working on this baby for a long time. I made a bunch of modifications as business has taken off. It's booming, now. I can't put out the stuff fast enough. So I'm thinking of expanding and bringing in some people to help. If you're interested, I'll give a discount. Say . . . ten percent."

She nodded. "How much is it?"

He held up a single, small bag. "This right here's three-hundred. It's the smallest I do. Depending on how much you need, this'll usually get you through the week, at least. You'd pay six?"

"Yes. Of course."

"Okay. We have a deal."

Mia winced. She didn't have any cash on her at all, not even just to flash at him, to get him to put his guard down. "Good to know. I'll have to get the cash together."

His proud smile fell. "You don't have cash?"

"No, but I'll get it," she said with an air of confidence, quickly changing the subject. "What if I want to sell? I have a couple people I know would be interested."

That seemed to appease him. "That's a discount, too. Ten percent. But if you get caught, I'm not involved. If I hear you putting my name out there, we'll never do business again, and you'd better watch your back. I have some pretty powerful friends. You catch what I'm saying?"

"I understand." She looked around at the various chemicals with interest. "So all of this stuff goes into making the drug?"

He nodded. "Yep. Not bad considering I failed chemistry in high school," he said. He really seemed to be excited to show it off to her. "I'll tell you, my stuff is worth every one of those three-hundred dollars. It's not some shit that's mixed with shoe polish or fillers. It's premium."

"It must be hard making the stuff, and dealing, too."

"Yeah. Dealing's not my favorite. Dealing with meth heads and their excuses? I'm done with it."

"You ever have anyone who won't pay?" she asked.

"Oh yeah," he said, and whistled. "All the time. What you got to do is get tough with them. Usually, just telling them they'll be cut off is enough to light a fire under them. They'll sell their own kids in order to get more of it. That's the beauty of it."

"But if they still won't pay?"

He shrugged. "Well, then, I bring in the big guns."

"Big guns?"

"My associates."

She leaned forward, interested. Was that something he just said, or did he really have hitmen that did his dirty business for him. "Like who?"

He smiled at her. "I don't think I need to answer that."

"Well, I just heard about that girl who was murdered. At Cedar Arms. So I was wondering. The police said it had something to do with a drug debt, maybe."

His eyes narrowed. "Don't know nothing about that. Must've been a competitor of mine."

"You sure?" she asked, gauging his reaction closely. "My kids knew her. I think her name was Merry? Merry . . . Summerhill?"

He'd been wiping off a counter with a rag. His eyes went wide for a split second, and he stopped what he was doing. Then he started up again. "Doesn't sound familiar. When was this?"

"Few days ago. Friday night. She was stabbed."

"Friday . . ." he murmured, then his Adam's apple bobbed. He didn't meet her eyes. "Don't know nothing about that. Must've been one of my competitors."

He's lying. She knew it immediately. He wasn't a very good liar, because she noticed beads of sweat, forming at his hairline, and his body had gone stiff and less natural. "That's funny," she said, knowing this was going to set off alarm bells for him, "A few of the people in the trailer park said they saw someone who looked just like you, at her trailer, before she died. Demanding $300."

His eyes flashed to hers. "What the—who said that?"

She shrugged. "People. We all talk, around there."

"Who are you?" he demanded, reaching for the gun in his pants. "I think it's about time you—"

Before he could say more, she got there first, grabbing his gun, pointing at him.

He scowled and shook his fist. "Twice in ten minutes? Seriously? I'm not usually this stupid."

She snorted. "I beg to differ. And not just because you don't know how to handle the gun. You let a total stranger just step into your meth lab because you were so proud of it, you couldn't help it. That makes you seriously dumb."

His scowl deepened.

"You killed her, didn't you? Because she wouldn't pay? Right?"

He shook his head. "Who the hell are you? Who do you think you are, coming in here and—"

"I'm someone who cares about what happened to Merry Summerhill. And I want to know. Did you kill her?"

He shook his head and leaned against the counter. "Sorry. You have the wrong man."

"So you deny you went there?"

He took a deep breath and let it out. "Fine. I was there. She was one of my customers. I went there because she'd been over at my place in town Thursday night, and she'd swiped a bag on me. I wanted payment." He swallowed. "I didn't know she was dead until just right now, when you told me."

"What happened?"

"What do you mean, what happened? Yeah, I came there at around midnight and knocked on her door, demanding my money. We had words. She pulled a gun and forced me out. I told her I'd be back and left on my bike."

"Did you come back?"

"No. I was going to. In a few days, though, once I gave her the time to collect the money, I was planning on sending my boys. Not right away. I went to the Double R Bar and got loaded instead, found a woman and brought her home at closing."

"You have anyone who can vouch for that?"

"Whole bar. Just ask them. I'm sure it's on their video cameras." He shook his head as a sudden thought came to him. "Shit. That means I'm never going to collect that money. That friend of yours has put me through a hell of a lot of trouble, you know that?"

"I'm really sorry," she said, her voice dripping with sarcasm.

But she *was* sorry, because she had the feeling she had the wrong guy. Though he was a lowlife, and not that bright, he seemed sincere. Plus, would someone really risk life in prison over a measly $300? She didn't think it seemed logical. "Did you see anyone while you were leaving?"

He shook his head. "No . . . you know, you sound like a police officer."

"I'm not. I'm just someone who wants answers."

"This ain't the place to be nosy. And if I hear you're going around, telling people what you saw here—"

"I won't. Like I said, all I care about is finding out what happened to Merry."

He looked around at his meth-cooking set-up and smacked his lips together. "So I guess our business is done here. Get out of here," he snarled.

"With pleasure," she said, backing away, not quite sure where to go now that this had become a dead end.

She left the cabin and dropped his gun on his property on the way out, so that he'd have to work to find it, later. Then she walked the mile back to the Cedar Arms trailer park, which gave her plenty of time to decide on her next steps. The only thing she could think to do, as the sun sunk lower in the sky, was to keep interviewing people in the park.

Someone had to have seen the person who climbed in Merry's window, after Mick left on his motorcycle. And since nobody in the park seemed forthcoming with information, she would just have to hunt that person down herself.

CHAPTER THIRTEEN

Mia was definitely in need of a change of clothes by the time she approached the arch over the entrance to Cedar Arms. It was at least ninety degrees, humid, and the jeans and t-shirt she'd been wearing for days practically clung to her sweaty frame. If Shilah would let her, she'd take fifteen minutes to grab those clothes from Merry's place, take a long shower, and then continue on with her interviews.

She also really wanted a glass of water. As she arrived at Shilah's trailer, licking her chapped lips, she saw an unfamiliar car parked near the office at the front of the building. This one, she would've remembered. It was sleek and black, and shiny, despite all the dust everywhere. A Mercedes S-Class, it stood out like a sore thumb. She'd definitely have remembered it if she saw it before.

Her heartbeat sped up.

The Marshals. They've found me.

That was her first thought. As she slowed her pace and made sure to cling to the shadows so that she wasn't in full sight of anyone who might be peering out the office windows, she rationalized.

Don't get too excited, yet, Mia. There's nothing to worry about until there's something to worry about.

She made it to Shilah's trailer and climbed the steps quickly, rapping softly before opening the door.

The first thing she saw was Rocky, sitting at the breakfast bar, a container of peanut butter in front of him. He had a spoon slathered with the stuff, his cheeks full. He looked up at her, stuck his pink, peanut-butter-coated tongue out, and licked the spoon.

"Hey, Rocky," she said kindly, offering him a smile. "Your mom around?"

He grunted and motioned toward the hallway with the bedrooms.

"Thanks," she said, heading that way. She found Shilah standing in Mia's guest room with a pile of clothes.

As she approached, Shilah lifted up a belly-baring camisole with spaghetti straps and hardly any material. "Then again," Shilah said, wrinkling her nose. "You might not appreciate Merry's style."

"Oh—you went back to her place?" Mia asked, sifting through the pile of clothes.

"Yeah, when I got back from dropping off Mrs. Mussman's prescription and groceries, I had a little time so I went over and picked out a few clothes. But I'm not sure if any of this will work," she said, lifting out a skin-tight bustier.

Mia found an oversize t-shirt and a pair of shorts. "This should be fine," she said with a smile.

"That reminds me," Shilah said, grabbing a Wal-Mart bag. "I thought you'd need these. I hope they're okay. I guessed your size."

Mia opened it to find a new package of underwear and some tank-style bras. "This is great. Thanks so much."

Shilah pointed down the hallway. "The shower's open for you, if you want. There are towels on the shelf outside."

"Thanks."

She turned to leave, and Shilah said, "Oh, what happened at that dealer's place?"

Mia shook her head. "No go. He has an alibi, and he didn't even know she'd been killed. Long Face had said he heard him leave. Someone else must've come in after he left."

She frowned. "Oh, no. Who could've done that, then? Merry might have gotten involved with some bad people, but she wasn't a bad person. She was helpful! If anyone ever needed a babysitter, she was there."

Mia nodded. "So she babysat for a lot of people around the neighborhood?"

"Oh, yeah. All over. Ever since she was a teenager. She babysat dozens of kids." She sighed. "She was so good with them. The kids loved her. So who would do this?"

That was a potential avenue—if she was so well-known in the area, maybe there was someone in the neighborhood she'd upset. Maybe someone who wanted drugs, and thought she might have them, though the place hadn't been ransacked. All the more reason to conduct more interviews around the area, if she could find anyone willing to answer questions.

"Oh," she said as she remembered what she'd wanted to ask Shilah in the first place. "Did you see that car out in front of the office?"

Shilah looked up from folding the clothes into neat squares. "What car?"

“The fancy black Mercedes. I was wondering who it could belong to. I have this Marshal who—"

“Oh, Honey. Don’t worry about that. It’s no one looking for you,” she said with a smile, patting Mia’s shoulder. “It’s Percival Wilton the Third.”

Mia leaned against the door jamb as she cradled her clothes against her chest. “Who’s that?”

“Percival Wilton. Some bigshot out of Dallas. He owns most of the real estate between here and the city. He also owns that big tract north of there. You probably saw it as I was driving you in?”

Mia relaxed, glad it had nothing to do with her first paranoid thoughts. She had plenty of other things on her mind, but during the drive to the park, she vaguely remembered seeing a yellow sign advertising a new housing development with pretty large McMansions. They seemed a bit out-of-place considering all of the trailer parks that were in the area. “Oh, that one with the big COMING SOON sign on it?”

“That’s it. Four-thousand acres. He’s in the process of developing it, but there’s one problem standing in his way.”

“What’s that?”

“Cedar Arms. It’s the closest trailer park to the development and it stands between his land and downtown. He thinks we’re an eyesore. So he keeps trying to sweet-talk our owner, Sal Bradford, into selling. So far, Sal hasn’t caved. He ain’t gonna.”

“And yet this developer keeps negotiating with him, so he must think there’s a chance, or he wouldn’t waste his time.”

“True. Sal’s hard as nails. Tells us he just likes listening to the blowhard up the ante. Sal says he never will sell, but—” She shrugged. “Everyone has their price. Wilton’s been here a dozen times in the last year. Maybe today’s the day he finally gets lucky.”

“I hope not, for your sake. Where would you move?”

Shilah sighed. “That’s the trick, isn’t it? Even if I got compensated for the two lots I own, it wouldn’t be enough to go anywhere else. Not by a long shot. But I doubt Sal will sell. He’s not interested.”

“Well, I hope it doesn’t go through,” she said, noticing something on Shilah’s face. Shilah was looking down, a crease growing in the center of her forehead. Something was on her mind, and it seemed deeper than just the remote possibility of losing her home. “Are you okay?”

She nodded. "I just thought of something, though. It's probably nothing. But a few months ago, right when I got out of prison, I stopped by Merry's home and saw Percival leaving."

"You did?"

"Yeah, it sure was odd because I had no idea they knew each other. I asked Merry what it was about and she made some excuse—I can't remember what it was, something about how he wanted a bottle of water, but it sounded like a lie. Because why would Percival Wilton stop in to see Sal at the front of the development, then go all the way to the back of the park to get a bottle of water from Merry? I just assumed maybe he was walking the perimeter of the land to see how big it was, so I let it drop. But now that I think about it, I don't believe it at all."

"Why don't you?"

"Because he was out of breath, and she was out of breath, and flushed, and I couldn't help thinking I'd interrupted some kind of romantic bang-bang, if you know what I want to mean." She wrinkled her nose. "Not exactly something I want to think about, my little sister having a thing with that man, but . . ."

Mia had been building a mental picture of this Percival Wilton the Third in her head—an old man with a top hat and monocle. Wealthy men of all ages had a penchant for young women, but the idea of this type of man having a possible affair with a woman like Merry seemed incongruous. "Wait—how old is this guy?"

"Thirty? Maybe thirty-five. He's young. Ambitious. Born with a silver spoon wedged up his backside. Kind of full of himself."

Mia adjusted her mental image of him and tapped on her chin. "Okay, so if they were having a relationship, do you think there's a reason he'd want her dead?"

Shilah shrugged. "Other than his wife and his kids?"

"Oh," Mia said, nodding. If Merry had threatened to tell his wife about the affair, it was possible.

She grabbed herself a towel on the way to the small bathroom, thinking. Once she finished with the shower, she'd stop by Merry's trailer. Maybe she could find some dirt on this Percival to confirm her suspicions.

*

Freshly showered and wearing her new clothes from Merry's wardrobe, Mia stepped outside Shilah's trailer, finger-combing her wet hair. As she did, she noticed the black Mercedes hadn't moved. Inside, she imagined the two players, neither of whom she'd met before, in the thick of negotiations. She had to wonder if the trailer park was closer to being sold than Shilah thought. If Sal had been adamant about not selling, surely the developer would've left by now?

She walked toward the back of the trailer park, noting that the people who were out in the early evening weren't much friendlier than they'd been when she first arrived. In fact, in the shadows, there were more of them, and they looked even more suspicious. She noticed a few mothers, watching their children play out front, who might be worth asking questions, but when she waved at them, they turned back without acknowledging her.

Tough crowd, she thought as she noticed a small group of young adults up ahead, sitting around a picnic table, drinking beers and laughing.

They stopped and glared at her as she walked past. For a moment, she though they might try something, and wished she had her weapon, but a few moments later, she heard them laughing again, saying something in Spanish about the *gringa.* They were laughing about her, but she could take that. At least they'd left her alone.

By the time she got to the back corner of the park, she'd shed the curious eyes of the other park residents. At least, she thought so. Though Miss Mussman's and Long Face's trailers were quiet, she knew they were in there, and could see lights from the windows of each.

Merry's, on the other hand, was utterly dark. Though she'd long since stopped being affected by murder scenes, a chill went through her as she climbed the steps. Something about the place seemed eerie, and being here alone, when there was a killer on the loose, was unsettling.

Pulling open the door, she turned on a light. She looked around, paying less attention to the place where the body was found and more to the other surroundings, specifically, places where she might find some connection between her and Percival.

She opened a drawer in the kitchen to find it full of utensils, a can opener, and a big, slotted cooking spoon. The next was the requisite "junk drawer" that every home seemed to have. Mia's, at her own home, was in the kitchen as well, and was for some reason always collecting her daughter Kelsey's hair ties.

Ignoring the stab of homesickness that threatened to derail her, she started to rifle through the assortment of pens, cards, papers, and unidentified doo-dads.

She opened a card with a bird on the front and read it: *Happy birthday, little sis. Don't know what I'd do without you! Love, Shilah and Rocky.*

It was dated a month before. Placing it back, she found a few more cards, snippets of paper with lists on it, an envelope from the electric company. Nothing too interesting. She pulled out a pad of paper and flipped through it, finding nothing but empty pages.

As she was about to put it back, she realized that the first page had indentations from heavy writing on it, from something that had been written on the now-removed page prior to it.

Squinting and lifting it up to the light so she could get the right angle, she noticed someone had written, *Hey, P* at the very top.

Percival? Possibly. And it looked like a letter.

Or at least, part of one. It only went on for a couple of sentences before cutting off, mid-page, with no signature. The handwriting was similar to that used for all the other lists and snippets in the drawer, so she assumed it belonged to Merry.

Tilting it again so she could read, she made it out:

Hey P,

If you think you can just break it off like that, you're wrong. I told you what I want and I'm not joking. I have proof. If you don't pay up, I'll tell

Mia smiled. Bingo.

Merry Summerhill had been blackmailing Percival Wilton the Third.

Grabbing the paper, folding it, and sticking it into the back pocket of her shorts, she quickly turned out the lights and left. But as she approached the front of the trailer park, she saw the taillights of the Mercedes as the car slowly navigated toward the exit.

Cursing, she swung around the front of Shilah's trailer and ran up the stairs. She burst in to find them sitting at the dinner table, food spread out in front of them, a third open seat and plate waiting for her.

"You're just in time," Shilah began. "I made chicken tetrazi—"

"Shilah!" she said, out of breath. "Can I borrow your truck?"

"Yeah," Shilah said, motioning to the door. "Keys are on the hook."

Mia looked up and grabbed them. "Thanks. Be right back."

She rushed out to the truck, started it, and threw it into gear. She had a millionaire to question.

CHAPTER FOURTEEN

Kane Wilcox leaned back in his chair and ran his hands down his face, feeling like he'd been hit by a truck. He was getting too old for this shit.

Right now, his wife Dana was in Corpus Christi, probably enjoying dinner with her friends. Since he was away most of the time, she'd managed to grow a healthy social circle of people she was close to. But none of those people knew Kane, and he didn't know them, either. He imagined if he did finally retire, he'd have to get to know them all, and that sounded like work in itself. Better to stick to what he knew, what he was good at. The job.

But though he'd been proud of his accomplishments in recent years, he couldn't say he felt that way, now.

It was because of Mia North.

He'd never gone this long without finding his man. Never. Usually the cracks were apparent within twenty-four hours after the escapee went on the lam. Mia may have been former FBI, so he knew that with her knowledge she'd be a challenge. But never did he think he'd still be looking for her, two months later.

As he finished rubbing his eyes, opened them, and focused on her former partner, Wilcox had to wonder if David Hunter was one of the reasons why.

Wilcox knew Hunter wasn't being entirely straight with him. He knew Hunter had something to do with her escape from that cabin up north, back when this ordeal began. He knew that Hunter had intel he wasn't being forthcoming about.

The only question was . . . how did he learn that information for himself?

When he focused on Mia's former partner, the man's eyes were narrowed, focused right back on him. Hunter was still suspicious of him, as well he should be. After all, Wilcox had been doggedly chasing after Mia, almost from the moment she broke free of the transport car on the way to New Mexico. And he'd nearly gotten to her.

But over the past few weeks, Wilcox had learned a thing or two about Mia. One—she was still solving crimes, despite being wanted by every law enforcement officer in the state.

Two—she wasn't going to go quietly.

Three—she had something tying her to the area, something more than just her family. Otherwise, she could've hopped the border, weeks ago.

No, she had a mind to prove she was innocent of this crime she'd been put away for. And so Kane didn't feel as though he'd have done his job well if he simply ignored that and brought her in. Try as he might, he couldn't simply cuff her and bring her in.

As a U.S. Marshal, no, it wasn't his business to care. But as a person, he did.

And he wouldn't be able to bring this woman in with a clean conscience unless he fully understood the crime she'd committed.

So as he sat there, with David Hunter's file on the Mia North case spread out in front of him, he felt like he was only at the mouth of a very deep rabbit hole.

"So, let me ask you this," he said as he turned the pages of another very thick file. "Who does she think actually killed Ellis Horvath?"

Ellis Horvath. According to his file, a very sick man. And, if Wilcox was being entirely honest, someone who didn't deserve to breathe air. The product of an unhappy childhood, full of abuse and hardship, he'd grown up to be the type who lived to cause chaos. He'd been put in jail for assault of a female at the age of seventeen, and his rap sheet just went on and on from there. Mia North had come in contact with him, apprehending him after he'd attempted to lure a child in a park. There'd been a couple of murders he'd been suspected of, as well.

But then it got dicey when Horvath, released on a damn technicality, went after her daughter. A couple of police reports were filed, but the asshole stayed on her, showing up at her school, following them home.

As the testimony from the murder trial went, Mia had just had enough of it, and had snapped.

She'd gotten a call from him, telling her to meet him in an abandoned warehouse in downtown Dallas, if she wanted this to end. She'd gone in without waiting for backup, and had shot him. At the time, he'd been unarmed.

David Hunter went through the files and pulled out a photograph. It was one he'd seen before, but somewhere else—on the front page of most Texas newspapers he'd seen on his travels. Everyone in Texas knew the senate hopeful Wilson Andrews. He had quite a lot of fans around the state.

Mia North was not one of them. The rumor was that she blamed him for the death of Ellis Horvath, and that he had framed her to stop her from investigating his brother, Jerry, another lowlife child predator.

"But all investigations into Wilson Andrews yielded nothing, or so I hear?" Kane said, his voice gravelly from too many cigarettes and too much caffeine.

"Zero."

"This here says that he was at an event elsewhere in the state during the whole Horvath incident."

Hunter scoffed. "You really think that guy would've pulled the trigger himself? No, he set him up, using this guy."

He handed him another photograph, of an unpleasant looking man with a dark moustache, in a Dallas police uniform. The name struck a chord, but he couldn't quite place it. "Kevin Reynolds . . . so it was an inside job?"

"Right. It's no secret Andrews has friends in high places. He has friends in the Dallas police, and Mia told me she uncovered some kind of connection between the two of them. Then what do you know . . . Reynolds winds up dead. Murdered."

Wilcox raised an eyebrow. "Murdered? When?"

"Couple weeks ago. You probably remember?"

He did, now that Hunter mentioned it. Reynolds had been butchered in his apartment, investigation ongoing. He remembered it because he'd tracked Mia to the area of Reynolds's neighborhood, at around the same time that he'd been found murdered. "And they don't have any suspects in that murder, I'm assuming."

"Nope. But Mia found out. It was some guy, some hitman, Ernesto something. But all he said was that there was a case involving some girl. Something had happened to a girl, and Reynolds felt bad for not reporting it. But it involved Wilson Andrews. That was all."

Wilcox nodded. "So that was why she was at his place then, yesterday? Confronting him? Did she really think he'd confess?"

Hunter threw up his hands. "I don't know why. It was a hell of a chance. I think she's getting desperate. She just wants this over. That's all. She's tired, and she wants to go home."

That was one thing Wilcox had going for him. She was getting desperate. And desperate people made mistakes. Or, even if she didn't make a mistake, she might be more apt to trust him. He needed a way to prove to Mia that he was on her side. And the only way he could do that was by convincing her ex-partner of the same thing.

Right now, it seemed as though it was starting to work. David was starting to be more open to him, slowly and surely, theorizing what might be going through Mia's mind.

If they knew that, then they'd find her.

Still, Kane was sure the man wasn't telling him everything. "All right. So how can we get her comfortable enough to meet with us?"

David scoffed. "Sorry, guy. That's not happening. The only way she'd meet with you would be if she was finally proven innocent and all charges were dropped against her."

Wilcox scratched at his temple. That wasn't happening. "That's not going to happen unless she cooperates with us. Isn't there some way to get her that mes—"

"I told you. I have had no contact with her in weeks."

Bullshit. It was almost written on Hunter's face in big, block print. "You're telling me you have no way of getting in touch with her at all. None?"

He leaned forward, palms flat on his desk. "I think I already told you that. Repeatedly."

He closed his eyes. Why did he feel like, with this guy, all he was doing was running around in circles? Maybe that was by design. Maybe Hunter wanted to tire him out.

A thought came to him. "We know she's intent on solving crimes in the area, big, high-profile ones, even though she's a wanted woman. So it stands to reason that she's somewhere near a crime . . ."

"So all we need to do is look over all of the many hundreds of open crimes that have taken place in Texas, recently." Hunter grinned. "Good luck with that."

"Some of the crimes she solved can be tied to her past. That last one, the one with the traveling circus, one of the victims was a son of a neighbor from the University Park area. Did you know that?"

Hunter shook his head.

"Yeah, I made that connection, a little bit after the killer was found. Turned out that she visited the victim's mother while she was a wanted woman. Took a hell of a chance going into her old neighborhood," he said. He'd been proud of himself for that find, but now, it seemed insignificant. "So it stands to reason that she might have a similar connection to whatever crime she might be interested in, now."

David snorted as he took a sip from his coffee. He hadn't offered Wilcox any, but Wilcox didn't mind. Though they were alike in a lot of ways—extremely suspicious—they weren't friends. Probably never would be.

He swallowed and said, "Only problem is, people like you, me, and Mia are friends with those who *solve* crimes. What I mean is, in the social circles we travel in, crimes don't happen that often. I'm sure that circus case was just an isolated one. I doubt you'd find another that she has a personal connection to."

He thought about it. True, most people in his own life lived relatively crime-free, thankfully. Suddenly, though, he sat up, as a thought occurred to him. "Yeah, but Mia, lately, hasn't been traveling in the same circles." He sifted through the paper.

David watched him. "What are you looking for?"

"I want details of who she was with in prison. People she was seen with. Do we have that information?"

"Yeah, somewhere, I guess, we had the name of her cellmate," David said, helping. "But why? What difference does that make?"

"Because maybe we could interview the cellmate. Maybe they've been in contact. Maybe she has an idea of crimes she might have an interest in."

David chuckled. Sure, it was a long shot. But right now, it was the only shot they had. "You really think that's going to do anything?"

Right then, Wilcox spotted the paper. It was a photograph of a large woman with a boyish, almost buzzed haircut and dark slivers for eyes, practically swallowed up by her large, puffy cheeks. Shilah Summerhill. He picked it up and stared at it. "Here. I found it."

Hunter said nothing for a long time. "Waste of time. There's no telling they even spoke."

As far as Wilcox was concerned, it was worth a shot. In fact, it meant there was someplace that he hadn't yet looked into, where Mia North could possibly be holing up. And that was good enough for him. "But maybe they did."

And it wasn't far away. Cedar Arms trailer park, twenty minutes to the east of Dallas.

He scribbled down the address and nodded. "I'm going to check it out tomorrow morning," he said. "You're welcome to come along, if you'd like."

Hunter shrugged and looked away. "What the hell. Sure, why not? I still say it's a big waste of time."

Wilcox smiled. Why did he get the feeling that Hunter was trying to put him off the trail, once again?

CHAPTER FIFTEEN

Mia drove in Shilah's old pick-up, past trees and more trees, trailer parks scattered among them, until they gave way to a town, and near the lake, larger and larger mansions. She tailed the Mercedes as she'd been taught in the academy, giving a good space cushion so as not to alert the driver. Thankfully, there were many other cars on the road, and by the time she drove into the nicer part of town, it was almost fully dark.

The Mercedes stopped at a light, and she pulled up, a car behind him. The windows were slightly tinted, but even so, she could see him, pounding the heel of his hand on the steering wheel to the rhythm of whatever song he was listening to on his radio. He had his window down, his arm hooked out, and seemed more interested in the blonde in the car next to him than in whatever was behind him.

A moment later, he pulled into a development of new, sprawling lakefront resort homes. A garage door at one of the houses began to rise, and he eased into the driveway, disappearing from view.

She pulled to the curb and watched the garage door close.

Then, she stepped out of the car and made her way up the path to the front door, past manicured hedges and a lawn so perfect, it looked like a green carpet. The brick-faced home towered over her, looking even more massive, the closer she got to it. Though it was a beautiful home, there was something about it that seemed cold and clinical.

She pressed the doorbell, and when she heard it ring inside, a child's voice said, "The door!"

A faraway female voice said something unintelligible, and then there was a scraping at the door. A second later, it opened a crack and a child's eyes poked out, near the doorknob, staring at her.

"Hi . . . uh, what's your name?"

The kid pushed the door open, revealing a little girl in a princess dress. "Minnie."

"Minnie, can I talk to your dad?"

The girl's eyes widened. Then she screamed. "Eddie!"

An older, Hispanic woman came rushing down the stairs, wiping her hands on her apron. "*Si*?"

"I'm looking for Percival Wilt—"

"What's this noise? Eddie, I told you to keep things down during my Peloton workout. Who is i—" a voice at the top of the stairs called, but suddenly halted.

Mia looked up to see an impossibly slim woman in a bra top and shorts, patting her forehead with a fluffy towel. When she removed it, there was a blonde, tanned, supermodel face, scowling down at her.

She groaned. "We don't need any. Eddie. Did you tell her we don't need any?"

The housekeeper attempted to respond but Mia spoke over her. "I'm not selling something. I'm looking for Percival Wilton. Your husband?"

"He is," she said with a sigh. "What do you want him for?"

"It's a business matter."

"Well, he's not home."

"Funny, I saw his car pull in a few minutes ago."

Her scowl deepened. "What are you doing, spying on our house? Well, you can just go f—"

"That's enough, Lane," a voice said inside the bedroom she'd just stepped out of. She turned toward the door, sufficiently quieted, then stepped aside to let a man step out.

The man was huge, bigger than she expected. His every step down the staircase made it groan. He wasn't just wide, but tall, too, well over six-five. When he stepped to the door, though, his voice was gentle. "I've got it, Eddie," he said kindly to her. "You can go help the kids."

As the little girl and the woman headed down a long, columned hallway with crystal chandeliers, he turned his attention to Mia.

"What is this about?"

"I'm from Cedar Arms Trailer Park," she said, to which his eyes widened. "Is there somewhere we can speak in private?"

He nodded excitedly. "Absolutely. Sal told me he would send someone with his decision in a few days, but I had no idea he'd make it this quickly. Are you his lawyer? You look like he caught you in the middle of something, huh?" he pointed to her plain t-shirt and shorts and then opened the double doors to a modern office, right off the main foyer. "You want something to drink?"

"No, that's fine," she said, slipping into a sleek metal chair across from the glass desk. "This won't take very long."

"All right," he said, sitting at the desk and lacing his fingers in front of him. He was a good looking man, who clearly worked out, with a short dark goatee and an expensive suit. "Let's hear it. You have an offer or not?"

"Actually," she said with a widening smile. "I'm not here on behalf of Sal."

His smile fell. "Excuse me?"

"I'm not here about the deal you're looking to do." He still looked confused, so she continued, "The development deal? That's not why I'm here."

"All right," he said, still sounding confused. "But didn't you say you were from Cedar Arms? So what . . . I don't get it."

"I'm here on behalf of someone else. Someone who isn't able to be here herself."

When his eyes narrowed, she saw the slightest crack appear in his confident façade. "You're speaking in riddles. Who do you mean?"

"Merry Summerhill."

Now his eyes narrowed further. "Merry . . ." He shook his head. "Don't know her. Sorry, but I think you've gotten the wrong idea. I can't help you."

"She lived in the back of Cedar Arms, in the pink trailer."

He snorted. "Sorry but I'm not an expert in the different residences there. As far as I'm concerned, they're all junk, so when I look at them, I imagine what they'll be when they're leveled to the ground, if you know what I mean. I don't—"

"I know a few people who'd say otherwise. In fact, they'd say you know that trailer very well, as well as Merry. Maybe that you even had a relationship with her?"

He threw a fist down against the glass table. "Bullshit. Who said that?"

"A few people who saw you there."

"Well, they're lying."

"Are they? Because I was in the trailer and saw some letters she'd written that have your name on it. Not to mention that you're on her contacts list in her phone," she bluffed. "So it does look a little suspicious, don't you think?"

His eyes were definitely wider now, and his fingers tapped on the glass. "Why have you been going through her things? What . . ."

"She was murdered. I thought you knew?"

His eyes finished widening. "No, I was out of state for the past week, in North Carolina, finishing up a deal there," he breathed. "Hell. Murdered?"

Mia nodded. "And the police have reason to believe she might have been blackmailing you."

He swallowed and shook his head. "No. She didn't blackmail me. I swear."

"She didn't? We found a note among her belongings that seemed to suggest . . ."

"Well, if she wrote a note, she never sent it to me. I never gave her any money."

She reached into her pocket and pulled it out, setting it in front of him.

"What, is it written in invisible ink?"

"No," she said, tilting it toward the light. "This isn't the original, this is the sheet that was under it on the pad. It clearly is written out to someone named P."

He squinted. "I guess I'm not P. And it's only half-written. Maybe she decided not to go through with it and tossed it. Or else it's someone else. She had a lot of men going in and out of there. It was like a revolving door, if you know what I mean."

"So you did have a relationship with her?"

He looked toward the door, and his family. Then he leaned forward, his voice soft. "No. I met her during one of my visits while I was checking out the land. She invited me in and we got to talking, and we came to an arrangement. I gave her money for information on Sal. She was pretty heavily messed up. With drugs. So she wasn't in any position to say no. But it only lasted a few weeks, and then I cut her off."

"Did she know that?"

"Yeah, she did. I told her I was looking for allies. I was trying to find ways to soften Sal up, and I thought she could help me. But it wasn't doing any good and so I realized I'd have to try something else. So I told her no more."

"And how did she take that news?"

"I thought it was okay, at first. I mean, she was upset, and we had a big fight, and when I left, she made a big stink, said she'd tell my wife I was cheating on her. But after that, we didn't have any contact at all. I swear, I haven't seen her in a month."

Mia eyed him, looking for any sign that he might be lying. But there was none. "I've heard you've come back several times to talk to Sal since then. You mean to tell me you never saw her while you were there?"

"Never. Not once. She was in the back of the development so I could avoid her. I didn't even know what she was up to." He threw up his hands. "And I didn't care to know. I never lied to her."

He did seem sincere. Not only did he also seem too big in size to be able to squeeze through the trailer window, he likely wasn't even in the state when the murder occurred. "And you say you were in North Carolina when it happened?"

"What day did it happen?"

"Last Friday."

He nodded. "Then yeah. I got back Sunday evening. I can give you the names of everyone I met with, if it'll. . . wait." He stared at her. "Who the hell are you? You're not the police, then why are you asking all these questions?"

"I'm a friend of her family," she said, standing up. "And I'm looking for answers."

He shrugged. "You're not going to get them here. There's the door. And I don't appreciate you coming here."

She nodded. "And we don't appreciate you coming to Cedar Arms. So if you know what's good for you, you might want to stay away. You understand?"

He scowled and pointed for the door. "Are you threatening me?" he said, reaching for his phone. "You're the one who is trespassing. I think I might just call the police. . ."

She rushed for the exit and escaped out into the night without seeing the rest of his family. He wasn't the killer. But right now, she had to get as far away from here as possible.

CHAPTER SIXTEEN

When Mia returned to Shilah's trailer, it was after eleven.

She parked the old pick-up in front of the house, but didn't get out right away. She looked around in the darkness, knowing that this was closer to how the park had looked when Merry Summerhill was murdered.

Despite the late hour, people were outside their homes, congregating in groups in the shadows. It looked like an outdoor party, with young people holding beers, listening to loud music. Nearby, some was setting off fireworks. Even kids were running around, dodging the trailers, playing tag. Though there were only a few lights here and there, the place seemed to come alive, much more so than in the day.

If this was how it had been the night Merry had been killed, someone had to have seen *something*.

The only question was, where to begin?

Just then, a woman laughed, loudly and jarringly, somewhere among the group. They all seemed to be having a great time. Mia had a feeling, though, that the second she stepped in and started asking questions about Merry, their attitudes would change.

So, yawning, she decided to call it a night. She hadn't slept in a nice, comfortable bed in what felt like a very long time. Maybe she could catch up on some needed rest.

As she climbed the stairs and put her hand on the doorknob, wondering if she should knock, she heard a voice inside scream, "Leave me the hell alone!"

She pushed open the door to find a similar scene to one she'd witnessed earlier in the day. Rocky was sitting in front of the television, eyes glazed, game controller in hand as he stared at the screen. This time, though, Shilah, standing over him, looked less indulgent. Her face was red, and she was shaking her head with her hands on her hips.

She looked up at Mia and shrugged. "I just told him it was bedtime."

Mia gave her a half-smile. Kelsey, though a few years younger, had always been stubborn about bedtime, too. She had to wonder how Aiden had been managing it, in the months since she had been gone. He'd never complained about it. Mia had to wonder if her daughter had changed. A bolt of pain shot straight through her heart—she didn't know. It was almost as if she didn't know her own daughter, anymore.

"In a minute, Mom, I said!" Rocky snarled, pulling his legs up under him. "Not now!"

She sighed and stepped over him, heading toward the kitchen as she wiped her hands on a towel. "It's Merry's fault. He had that console in his bedroom at her place. But I'm afraid if I let him take it in there, I'll never see him again."

Mia wiped at her eyes. "I'm really tired. Thinking of turning in."

"Sure. Where have you been?"

She blinked and then realized she hadn't told Shilah anything about her theory regarding Percival. "Oh, it was a bust. But I had to track the lead down, just to make sure."

"You thought Percival Wilton might have been involved, didn't you?"

She nodded. "I found a paper in Shilah's trailer that made me think she might be blackmailing him. So I went to Wilton's house to ask him about it."

Her eyes went wide. "So was he involved?"

"I don't think so. I mean, obviously, he denied it all, having that family of his. But he also told me he was out of state during the murder, in North Carolina. Not to mention that he's rather big. I don't see a guy like him easily getting through that bedroom window."

"Oh," Shilah said, eyes downcast. "Maybe it really was just a random murder."

"You said there have been other crimes in the park? Other murders?"

She nodded. "There was a shootout, a couple months ago, right when I got out of prison. Gang related. A couple kids got shot. One died."

"Yes, but anything similar to Merry? Where the murderer was never caught? Maybe chalked up to drugs?"

She shook her head. "Not here. Not that I can think of. But there are other parks in town that have the same problems. I seem to remember a murder that happened somewhere . . . an old lady? But that was before I went to prison."

She made a mental note of that one. It might be a good idea, if this park didn't pan out, to ask about crimes in nearby neighborhoods. Of course, it would've been so easy if she was still on the force. She could've just plugged in a few parameters, and *voila*—a list of similar crimes would be right there at her fingertips. But she didn't have access like that, and David was now completely unreachable. She'd have to do the legwork herself.

Tomorrow.

As she walked toward her room, Shilah followed, then reached behind the television set and yanked the plug out of the wall.

"Hey!" Rocky shouted as the screen went dead.

"I told you. Bedtime," she said, dropping the cord. "It's late. Get a move on."

He scrambled to his feet. "You're a wicked bitch!" he snarled at her, throwing the controller on the ground and stomping past them.

Shilah rolled her eyes. "The joys of raising children."

Mia let out a laugh, but it was a mournful one. She wished that she could call and hear her daughter's voice. Anything. Even if her daughter called her a wicked bitch, it would be something.

She said goodnight to Shilah and went into her bedroom. Shilah had folded and placed all of Merry's clothes into a dresser across from the bed. She opened it and rummaged through, finding an oversized nightshirt, which she changed into. Climbing back on the bed, which was soft and a bit uneven, but comfortable, she let her head fall against the pillow and closed her eyes.

Moments later, she was dreaming. She knew she was dreaming, because Aiden and Kelsey were there, and yet every fiber of her body was pushing her to believe that it was real. She wanted it to be real. She and her family, walking up and down the aisles of a craft fair, as they sometimes did on lazy Sunday afternoons. Kelsey was toting a blue balloon and licking the top of a strawberry ice cream cone, excitedly taking everything in.

And Mia wasn't taking a single thing for sale in. All she could do was marvel at her family. Here. Close. It felt so good to be with them again, it brought tears to her eyes.

"Mommy, Daddy, can I get a pretzel?" she asked, pointing with the finger that had the balloon string coiled around it.

"I think you've had enough treats for one day," Mia said, as a shadow from the clouds fell over them, darkening the area around them.

"Oh, come on, one pretzel won't hurt her," Aiden said, fishing in his pockets for change. "I'm hungry, too."

Mia shrugged and let them head off toward the pretzel cart, and that was when she noticed something interesting. At one of the booths, a salesman was calling, his voice, high and lilting, "Never before seen, don't miss your opportunity to be a part of this special sales event." A small crowd was gathered around, mesmerized by whatever this man was selling.

She moved closer, expecting to see the usual—jewelry or cleaning solution or candles or bath soap, all the stuff people usually peddled at these places. As she drew closer, she saw that the salesman was none other than Long Face—though not the Long Face she'd met earlier, but the one she'd conjured in her head, a cartoonish figure with a gaping mouth and a jaw that stretched to the ground. He was wearing striped pants and a shiny vest, like a carnival barker.

The crowd dispersed as he pointed to his wares, and she took them all in, with growing horror—the heads of criminals she'd apprehended in the past, bloody and staring at her with menacing eyes.

"May I draw your attention to this one," the barker said, pointing to a face that looked very much like her own.

Gasping, she whirled, only to realize the crowds of people had turned into shambling, decaying zombies.

And where was her family?

A bolt of relief shot through her as she spotted them, walking together through the next aisle over. Kelsey pointed something out excitedly, oblivious to the zombies creeping past her.

"Kelsey! Aiden!" she shouted out, stumbling to reach them. But as she made her way to the aisle, she found no passage through. Though she could see them quite clearly as if looking through a window, there was no way to get to them at all. Every time she stepped around a booth, there were boxes in the way. Or a beehive. Or a horde of bloodthirsty zombies.

She kept trying, growing more and more frantic and frustrated, until her voice was nearly lost from screaming and shouting her family's names. They never turned, never looked back. They continued on, munching on their pretzels, a spring in their steps, as if they were perfectly happy without her.

She shouted again for them, but suddenly, something slipped around her ankles, holding her back. She looked down to find two giant vines, entwining around her legs, tightening as they tugged her backwards. Kicking and squirming to free herself only made them tighten faster, and then she found herself being dragged away from her family.

Reaching for them, she screamed and gasped as the vines climbed up her body, threatening to swallow her whole as they pulled her farther and farther away, past the booths of the arts and crafts fair. Within seconds, she could barely see them.

"Aiden! Kelsey!" she cried, but by then she could no longer see them.

She sprang up in bed, the sheets twisted around her legs, breathing hard. There was a cold sweat on her forehead, and her t-shirt clung to her trembling frame. Looking around, she took in the blank walls and boxes piled up in Shilah's spare bedroom, and slowly, her breathing returned to normal.

It had just been a nightmare. But that didn't mean Kelsey and Aiden weren't out there, suffering just as badly as she was. Aiden had pushed on for Kelsey's sake, trying to make life as normal for her as possible. But that day, the day Mia was arrested, had driven cracks into their happy family life, which only widened more, every day she spent away from them.

Those cracks would never be repaired, no matter how hard they tried. And even though she fought for it every day, there was a slim chance she'd ever be able to prove herself innocent and go home. Which was why sometimes she did think it was better if they learned to forget her, to move on without her. If they did, they might have a chance at a normal life. If they did, eventually, Kelsey might go off to college, have a family, and forget the pain of her childhood, of having a fugitive mother torn away from her when she needed her most.

But that didn't make it hurt Mia any less.

Pulling the sheets over her body and clinging them to her chin, she settled back into bed and closed her eyes. But, thinking of the dream, and of her family, moving on without her, she didn't fall asleep again for the rest of the night.

CHAPTER SEVENTEEN

By the time Cal Shoemaker finished partying it up with the rest of his boys, it was after two.

This was his life, and it was a good one. All the suckers from high school told him that he'd never make anything of himself, because he failed math and science and English class. That had been bullshit. He didn't want to be a stupid pencil-pusher, a bank teller, or some worthless job like that. They could have those jobs.

Now, he had a sweet BMW, his pockets were flush with cash, and he got all the tail he wanted. Half the park was addicted to his supply, so he had no shortage of customers. He was on track to afford one of those sprawling lakeside mansions in another year or two.

Not that he wanted to do that. He liked it here, with his homeboys, close to his clientele.

He finished the joint he was smoking and stubbed it out in front of his trailer. Then, taking a swig of his near-empty beer, he climbed the steps and went inside, petting his cat Twister. He tossed the bottle in the sink with the other empties, then opened his fridge and fished out another one.

Settling down into his recliner, he grabbed the remote and turned on the television, flipping the channels until he found an older Marvel movie. He kicked off his flip-flops, took a swig, and let his eyes fall closed. Usually, this was right where he slept, and he didn't mind it. So many of his friends had moved in with their girlfriends, but that wasn't him. *No hitch to a bitch,* he told his buddies when they asked. He smiled, thinking that none of those whipped assholes would ever be able to fall asleep in front of the television, not with their bossy girls ordering them around. He liked being alone, king of his domain.

Yeah, he had it pretty good.

As he was half-watching the television, letting the bottle droop into the space between the cushion and the arm of the velvet recliner as he began to nod off, there came a knock at the door.

He blinked awake, sure at first that he'd imagined it. Twister was sitting on the coffee table, though, ears perked, alert. She'd heard something.

Cal checked the clock. After three. "Who the hell could that be?" he mumbled, rising to his feet, wondering if it was Frankie. Frankie, down the street, had told him he needed some stuff and would be by asap. Cal hadn't thought this soon, but who knew? Maybe Frankie was desperate. The man had been a full-fledged heroin addict for years. Cal kept expecting his OD, any day now.

Ordinarily, he would've told Frankie to screw himself, come back tomorrow. But it was a thousand bucks he was talking about. He could manage.

Rubbing the bleariness from his eyes, he reached into the stash he kept in his coffee table, grabbed the plastic bag, and went to the door. Pulling it open, he said, "You weren't kidding me when you said you needed it right—"

He stopped when he realized he was talking to dead air. There was no one there. He stepped forward, poking his head out, searching up and down the dark road, wondering if that loser was playing a trick on him.

Then he turned, closed the door, and looked at Twister, who was now licking her side, grooming herself. Maybe she hadn't heard anything after all.

"Thanks for the false alarm," he muttered, tossing the bag into his stash.

He grabbed his beer, took another long drink, though it was getting warm. As he lowered himself into the chair, the sound came again. This time, it was definite—a quick rap on the door.

Cal growled. Frankie was a bit of an idiot. He was always playing games. Now, Cal was pretty sure the asshole was trying to play a trick on him.

Grabbing the stash again, he swung open the door. Again, there was nobody there. The trees across from him swayed in the wind, which whistled between the trailers. His eyes traveled over all the possible hiding spots, trying to find the guy, but he could see anything. He stared out into the darkness and said, louder than usual, so Frankie would hear, "Guess you don't want the stuff after all."

He waited a beat, sure the guy would come running, apologizing, the thousand dollars in hand.

Nothing.

"All right. Good night, Frankie," he said loudly, grinning sadistically as he closed the door with a loud clatter. *You can suck my left one, Frankie. Just for that, I'm making you wait until tomorrow.*

After all, it wasn't like Frankie could get the stuff from anyone else. He was the only heroin dealer in the area. Most people around dealt in meth, but he'd found his groove with the big H, and a dealer who brought the stuff right over the border from Mexico, and sold it to him pretty cheap. A lot of people had wanted a piece of his business, wanted to help him and share in his riches, but he'd told them all to go to hell. This was his territory.

And he was king.

As he stood there, leaning against the door, his vision went blurry, and Cal realized just how tired he was. Maybe he was getting older, and these late nights were catching up to him, but he needed the rest. It was time for bed.

He grabbed the beer, finished it, and tossed the bottle in the sink. Bending over to grab the remote and turn off the television, he heard it again.

Another knock.

He swung around and stared at the door. He saw something moving in the shadows through the front windows, showing that indeed there was someone there. It had to be Frankie. No one else would think to mess with him like this.

That guy has a hell of a lot of nerve.

Stalking over to it, he grabbed the handle and pulled the door open. "You'd better goddamn come out from the shadows before I smash your face in!"

Again, there was nothing. Nothing out there at all. Overhead, an owl hooted, but all of the other sounds—the laughing from the parties, the loud, thumping music, had disappeared, making the night feel slightly eerie.

He shrugged it off. Cal had grown up in this neighborhood, knew it like the back of his hand. He ruled this place. What he said, went. And he sure as hell didn't want some snot-nosed addict making a fool of him.

Looking around, he caught sight of his aluminum baseball bat in the corner of the living room. It had been a long time since he'd swung it.

In high school, he'd been varsity, one of the best players on the team. Seemed like a million years ago.

Maybe I should take it out, give it a few swings for the fun of it, he thought as he looked at it. It had dust bunnies clinging to it, meaning it definitely needed to get some time in. *And while I'm at it, I'll scare the crap out of Frankie.*

He picked it up and dusted it off slightly, then turned to the door and stalked outside. Casually taking the steps, he reached the bottom and looked right and left.

Branches cracked in front of him, near a line of bushes. Giving the bat a few good test swings, he smiled. He took a step that way, then heard a fragile mewling behind him.

Cal turned to find Twister looking at him curiously from the front step.

"Go inside, baby, this won't take long," he said, turning toward the bushes. They were thick, and there was no light at all, save for a slim shaft of moonlight, so the bushes in front of him looked like a solid black mass.

Stepping close, he took his bat and quickly shoved it in, shouting, "Take that!"

He expected to hit the firm but yielding surface of someone's body, and to hear an "Ow." But instead, the bat went through the bush, hitting something too hard to be human. A branch. As he stood on his toes, looking over the bush for anyone hiding behind it, he plunged the bat between the brambles at different directions, but found the same result. There was no one inside or behind the bush. It must've been a squirrel.

Spinning, starting to feel like he was being taken advantage of, he took another step and shouted, "Frankie, you're going to wish you'd never been born!"

He walked around the entire perimeter of the trailer, feeling more and more like a dunce. No one made him feel this way. When he got a hold of Frankie, forget about not giving him his stash. No, not only would he not do business with him again . . . he was going to rip his head off.

By the time he got back to the front of the trailer, he was gnashing his teeth. Partly because he was pissed at Frankie, but also because, he was starting to get a little nervous.

Not a lot. Just a little.

Frankie was a hardcore addict. He was heavy on his feet, a little dopey and clumsy, and when he was drunk—like he certainly was at the party, an hour ago—he usually knocked things over and stumbled into things. He wasn't some ninja. He wasn't this slick.

And if it wasn't Frankie . . . then who?

He was out of ideas. He had a lot of associates, a lot of friends, but no one so stupid as to pull this shit on him.

"I'll give you one last chance. Come on out," he called into the void, but the only sound in response was the leaves, rustling overhead.

He shook his head and stalked toward the door, where Twister was waiting in the open space, warm orange light from the living room spilling in from behind her.

He leaned down and gave her a pet as he came in, then muttered, "Same bullshit, different day," as he sealed the door. He didn't usually use the safety lock, but this time, he did. Just in case anyone was thinking of pulling any more funny business.

Cal looked around the place, as a thought came to him.

He'd left the door open when he went around the trailer.

Whoever had been outside . . . could now be *inside*.

He went over to Twister, studying her. She wasn't a guard dog by any means, but if there was someone else inside, she'd let him know. At least, he hoped that she would. But she looked just as bored with him as usual. Now that he was back inside, she lost interest in him, jumping onto the kitchen counter to the chair to the ground and making herself comfortable in her bed.

He yawned then rolled his eyes. This was a waste. He should be in bed now, asleep. The sound had probably just been the wind, the trailer settling after the rains they'd had, a couple days ago. That was all.

As he spun to head toward his bedroom, he turned off the light and in that brief second, saw a familiar face. He barely had time to register who it was before the figure lunged forward, blade in hand, driving it into his chest.

He let out a strangled cry and tried to remove it, tried to pull away, but by then, the blood was spreading rapidly across his t-shirt and the attacker was working to remove it himself.

But not to help him. The second the attacker got it loose, it was plunged in again, this time, deeper. This time, he could feel the knife scrape against this inside of his breastbone, feel the point puncturing his organs with a searing pain.

He knew he would not survive this. His instinct was to run, but his feet wouldn't perform the movement. His legs refused to obey, instead, folding beneath him, and he plunged to the kitchen floor, gasping for breath.

As his vision whirled, the attacker stepped over him, wiping the blade of the knife with a handkerchief, and heading for the door. The last thing Cal felt was Twister's soft pink nose, sniffing at his face with mild interest.

CHAPTER EIGHTEEN

Mia didn't sleep after her nightmare, but she didn't feel like getting out of bed, either.

She was tired. Tired in her bones, and in her head. She spent the rest of the night, staring at the ceiling, thinking about her nightmare, and dreading the idea of getting up. Here, at least, she was somewhat safe. Anywhere else, she wasn't. The thought of running away, now, made her head hurt. Her body, too. If she'd felt like this, all those months ago, when the corrections staff had initiated her transport to the New Mexico Correctional Center, she likely would've just sat there like a good prisoner and none of this would've happened.

In a way, it might have been easier. No, she'd never be back with her family again. But she wasn't seeing very much of them now, either. If she was stuck in prison, at least she'd get weekly visits.

Maybe she was doing all of this for nothing. Maybe she needed to give up.

Realizing her hope was draining, she murmured to herself, *Just a little more time. Just give it a little more time.*

Then, with great effort, she pulled herself up out of bed and went to the small window, peeking out. Though the screen captured and highlighted every last feathery grain of dust on it, beyond that, she could see a glorious day dawning. Beams of bright white light filtered down through the trees, like an aura cast down from the heavens.

Maybe it was a sign. A sign to keep holding on.

Since she needed all the hope she could get, she decided to take it as one. She went to the dressers, pulled out a tank top and a pair of jean shorts, and changed, then went out.

The living room was still quiet and still, the video game controller still lying in the center of the room, where it had been left last night. Likely, Rocky was asleep, and would be that way for another few hours at least.

The smell of fresh coffee perked her up instantly. She picked up the controller and set it by the television, something she would've done at home, and went to the kitchen, where she found Shilah sitting, watching the news on a small, under-the-counter-mounted television. She smiled when she saw Mia. "Hey, hope I didn't wake you?"

"No. Not at all," she said, heading for the coffee machine on the counter. "This up for grabs?"

"Sure is. Mugs in the cabinet above you."

She remembered that from when she'd had tea with Shilah the day before. She opened the cabinet and took a chipped green mug from the assortment of various drinkware, then set it down and poured a full mug, intending to drink it black.

When she turned, a newscaster was droning on about the sad state of the economy. She motioned to the television. "What's new in the world today?"

"Not much. Same doom and gloom. I don't know why I feel like I need to start my morning off with it. It always puts me in a bad mood," she said with a shrug, motioning to the stool across from her. When Mia sat, she said, "Do you have plans for today?"

Mia nodded. "Well, since my whole idea with Percival Wilton got blown up, I suppose I'm just going to walk around the park and ask questions, see if anyone will talk to me. Do you know of anyone else in the neighborhood she might be close with? They might not have seen anything that night, but they might know of someone who wanted her dead."

Shilah shook her head. "I don't know very much. Unfortunately, I was working so much since I got out that I didn't really take stock of all her friends. But like I said, she did like to sit for the neighborhood children."

That was helpful. Every time she'd walked through the neighborhood, she'd seen plenty of kids, running about, enjoying their summer vacation. So all she had to do was find a parent who Merry babysat for. *If* they were willing to talk to her. And judging by the glares she'd gotten from the parents, she wasn't sure how easy that would be.

"Okay, then that's what I'll do."

Shilah pulled herself up from the table. "Want breakfast? I was going to make bacon and eggs."

"That sounds great," she said as she sipped her hot coffee, savoring the bitterness on her tongue. She already felt a little guilty for almost giving up hope, last night.

There was always hope. She just had to find it.

For a brief moment, she wondered if David had unearthed anything. There were no bombshell accusations against Wilson Andrews on the news, even though she prayed for one every night. Sometimes she thought that was the only thing that would save her—that if Andrews got caught in another scandal he couldn't press buttons to pull himself out of, maybe society would finally change their tune and start looking into previous cases involving him.

No, as far as her own case was concerned, it was status quo.

Shilah clattered cookware in the cupboard, pulling out two giant fry pans. She set them on the stove and opened the refrigerator. As she pulled out eggs and a sleeve of bacon, she said, "I feel a little guilty, Mia, honestly. All the work you're doing to get to the bottom of Merry's death? Maybe I should just let sleeping dogs lie, but I want something better for Rocky."

She smiled. "Nonsense. You have no idea what you're doing for me, giving me a place to stay. You know, you could be in real trouble if the police found me here."

She snorted. "You think I care about that? I'll just tell them I had no idea."

Mia gave her a doubtful look. "You had no idea I was in prison? We were *cellmates*."

"I'll just tell them I thought you were released for good behavior from your new prison. That's all."

Mia clenched her teeth. It wouldn't be that easy. The police wouldn't buy it, and she'd be put in jail again. But this time, she'd have no one to look after poor Rocky. She was always putting her friends and family in so much danger, just associating with them. Again, she felt guilt jab at her, but she said nothing, turning instead to the television, where a weatherman was giving the local forecast.

Sunny and cloudless, eighty, a perfect summer day. If this was an ordinary summer, she and her family would be packing up for their summer vacation. They usually went to South Padre Island, but once, they'd gone up to the mountains in Colorado, where they spent the week learning how to ride horses. Kelsey, initially so afraid, had turned into a real cowgirl during that time. It'd been so fun, watching her grow up, right before Mia's eyes.

And now . . .

Her eyes misted over, but she shook it away and tried to concentrate on the news as the frypan sizzled and the smell of bacon filled the air.

Wrapping her hands around her mug, she was just about to take another sip when a serious voice on the news said, "We now turn to breaking news out of Gun Springs City. Law enforcement there found a body in the Gun Springs Trailer park earlier this morning . . ."

Shilah must've heard it, too, because she moved the frypan off the burner and her eyes narrowed. "Did they say Gun Springs?"

Mia nodded and turned it up, listening. "Police say a man has been stabbed. No suspects as of yet, and the victim has not been named."

Her eyes widened as an on-the-scene reporter in a pink suit stood in front of a trailer that looked nearly identical to Shilah's. "Yes, Doug," she said, touching her earpiece. "We're getting word right now that the victim was a white male in his twenties, and the murder was committed sometime last night. It's not the first crime to happen this summer, but it is the first murder, which is concerning neighbors."

The screen cut to an old woman with scraggly gray hair and a missing eye tooth, the microphone in front of her. "It's hard to believe, this," she spoke in a deep Southern drawl. "We don't get nothing like murders here. It makes all of us so scared. I live here thirty years and the place done gone to pot."

A voiceover said, "Neighbors are definitely on watch today. Though this area is known for fun and sun, because of the reservoir nearby, it's also become a haven for drugs and prostitution, as well as gang activity, in recent years, according to police chief John Smithers."

Then the screen cut to an older policeman with a bushy moustache. "Yeah, crime always goes up during the summer months when we get an influx of tourists, but it really has been skyrocketing in recent years, due to the availability of drugs coming over the border. We're seeing a lot more crime, especially violent crime like murders. Seems like every day we hear of another shootout. This one's different, the victim was stabbed, but we do have reason to believe it might be over drugs."

Then it cut back to the woman, who was standing, grasping her microphone, stone-faced. "As you can tell, a very difficult, harrowing situation out of Gun Springs Trailer Park, which will undoubtedly be on the minds of all of those headed to the Cedar Arms Reservoir this summer vacation season."

Stabbed. The victim was stabbed. And the killer is on the loose.

It could've been just a coincidence. After all, there were plenty of crimes being committed in the name of drugs around these parts. It might not have had anything to do with Merry's murder, but even so, the matching details stood out.

Mia turned to Shilah. "Gun Springs Trailer Park. Where is that?"

Shilah said, "Just down the street. Maybe a mile past that cabin you went to? Right before you get to town. It's smaller than this one, but . . ." She trailed off as she studied Mia. "You're thinking they might be connected?"

"They might be. I don't know why I wasn't thinking about it before, but your sister's murderer might not be limiting himself to Cedar Arms. He might have killed in other places, too. I think we need to widen our search."

Shilah nodded slowly. "Makes sense. So how?"

She pushed her coffee away and grabbed a nearby pad and pen. "You think you can give me a list of the local trailer parks in the area?"

Shilah began listing them out at once.

Mia started to write them down, and then realized it would be a good idea to look up any murders at all in the area. If only she hadn't had to ditch her phone. She said, "Do you have a phone?"

Shilah lifted hers from the counter, unlocked it, and set it down in front of Mia. Mia typed in: *Stabbing Gun Springs.*

A number of results came up, starting with several articles for this latest murder.

But now she felt like she was getting somewhere. She needed to start with the most recent murder. So when Shilah placed the plate full of eggs and crisp bacon in front of her, she dug in, hardly tasting it as her mind swirled with thoughts.

By the time Shilah sat down with her own plate, Mia was done. She took the plate to the sink to wash it off.

"Whoa," Shilah said, scooping up a forkful of eggs. "What's your rush?"

"I'm going out there," she said, pointing at the television. "To that Gun Springs Trailer Park. I'm going to see what I can find out."

Shilah's eyes widened and her eggs fell from the fork, onto her substantial chest. "Son of a bitch," she said, wiping it off. "But you can't go there, Mia. It's suicide. The police are probably swarming all over it."

She shrugged. "I actually have some experience in avoiding them."

Shilah scrambled off of her stool and grabbed a piece of bacon. "Well, then, hold up and wait for me. I'm driving you."

CHAPTER NINETEEN

David Hunter sat in the passenger seat of U.S. Marshal Kane Wilcox's SUV, nervously tapping his fingers on the door's armrest.

This wasn't good. Not good at all.

If only he'd had some way of getting in touch with Mia, telling her that trouble was on its way. But he didn't. He didn't even have Shilah's phone number, not that he would've been able to call her and warn her without Wilcox breathing down his neck.

So the best he could do was try to convince Wilcox that targeting Shilah Summerhill was a waste of time. So far, it hadn't worked.

"I don't know what you think she's going to tell you," Hunter said smoothly, yawning. "She just got out of prison herself a month ago. She's probably been focusing on her own problems. She has enough to do without worrying about Mia North."

"Mmm-hmm," Wilcox said with no interest whatsoever, pressing on the gas. Now, he was going near ninety as they cruised on the interstate toward Gun Springs City.

"Waste of time, if you ask me," he said for probably the twentieth time in an hour.

The Marshal snorted. "So you've told me."

"Because it is one. And I got a lot to do, back at the office."

He needed to stop doing that. He was protesting too much, making himself look all the more suspicious.

"You didn't have to come."

"Yeah, I did. If it involves Mia, I want to be there," he said, his voice low, tapping the armrest at a frantic pace, now. *Please don't be there, Mia. Please tell me you stopped in, decided you needed to take my advice and get as far away as possible, and are now sitting on a beach somewhere in Cozumel, drinking pina coladas.*

"Why, Agent Hunter," Wilcox said, turning to him slightly and looking at him over the top rim of his sunglasses. "Is it just me, or do you look nervous?"

David frowned and laid his sweaty palms flat on his thighs. He was trying his best not to look overly nervous, and failing. He could feel the sweat trickling down his ribcage.

But if he let Mia down again, he'd never forgive himself.

"Not nervous," he said. "Just worried about all the stuff I've got to do back home. I hope we can make this snappy because I need to pick up my kid from camp at noon."

"No problem," Wilcox said as they pulled up to the Cedar Arms trailer park. Despite a rather fancy, attractive arch at the front entrance, the moment they pulled through, he felt like they'd entered a war zone. There was a heap of scrap and other garbage, planted in front of a dirt lot, and across from that, a rusty trailer that had a faded sign on the door that said, OFFICE. The other trailers weren't in much better condition; it looked like every one of them was in a stage of decay, broken, bent, and covered in graffiti, with shaded windows, blocking out the sun.

"Geez, anyone still live here?" Hunter said, scanning the area. "Looks deserted."

He hadn't meant anything by it, but Wilcox scoffed again. "Get off it. I don't know why you're trying to get me to turn this car around, but we're here now, and we're looking into it."

"I'm not trying anything," he said, though the lie was pretty obvious. "There's number twelve. What number did you say Summerhill's was?"

"Sixty," he said, looking at a piece of paper.

He drove down an aisle at a slow speed, and as they went through, he noticed a few people outside. A man hunched over the open hood of his truck popped his head out to glare at them, banging his wrench against his palm in a warning. A couple of kids stopped playing cards atop a picnic bench to give them a similar icy reception. A few guys who looked like gang members leaned against the side of a trailer, smoking cigarettes, cold eyes following their every move. A woman hanging clothes on a line looked as if she was ready to spit on them.

"Well, this place sure is friendly," he remarked, wondering what the chances were that Shilah Summerhill would give them the same reception, and he'd simply take it, turn around, and go home.

Probably not good.

"Yeah, places like this—the ones where everyone's suspicious of everyone else? They are that way for a reason."

"And what's that?"

"They're hiding something," Wilcox said. "And we just need to scratch it out. Might take a little longer than most, but I'm up for it. Are you?"

He stared at Hunter, challenging him. He sighed. "Look, I don't know what this lead you're following is going to shake out. But if it does . . ." He stopped, collecting his words. "If it does, and if you find Mia North at the end of this, you have to promise me you won't just throw her in jail. You have to give her a voice, and listen to her."

He nodded.

"I told you, I will."

"There are far too many people in Wilson Andrews's back pocket. She needs friends. Better ones than me. I can only do so much," he said, annoyed by how weak and beaten his voice sounded.

"Got it. Like I said, you have my word."

He still didn't know what to believe, but he knew Mia had to have been tired of all this. After all this time, she would probably welcome some out-of-the-box thinking, since everything she'd tried so far had her running up against a brick wall. She wanted an out, and unless something big happened, maybe Kane Wilcox was her out. The only way they'd know if they could trust him was by feeling him out, seeing how he responded. This, he decided, was as good a test as any.

But it was also dangerous. If Wilcox wasn't a man of his word, and he found Mia here and slapped cuffs on her, it would all be over, and it would be David Hunter's fault.

They found the trailer near the front of the park. It looked quiet, all the shades drawn, and unlike the other homes, there was no car parked in front—just a small patio with a few old lounge chairs set up outside.

Wilcox jumped up and jogged to the door even before Hunter had gotten out. He couldn't help dragging his feet, but he had a worsening feeling that he was making a big mistake.

Wilcox rapped on the door, but there was no response. He rapped harder.

"No one home," Hunter said, not yet allowing himself to relax. Wilcox wouldn't give up this easily.

He rapped harder and harder, and then called, "Shilah Summerhill! This is the U.S. Marshal's Office. Open up."

No response. David looked over his shoulder to see a couple of young guys—more gang member-types—watching. He ran his hand over the butt of his pistol, under his jacket, and frowned.

"Hey, you want us to leave this trailer park alive?" Hunter said under his breath, motioning to the men. "Quiet down."

The Marshal looked them over and shrugged. "They want trouble from us? They can come and get it," he said, knocking more and shouting louder, "Open up before we break this door down!"

Again, there was no answer.

Wilcox backed up toward the edge of landing and faced his shoulder toward the door. "Stand back and let me at it."

Hunter stared at him. So they were going to do this thing. Make a scene and have every person in this neighborhood watching. Fantastic. He had the brawn, so ordinarily, he would've offered to do it himself, except for one thing.

He didn't want to be here.

Just as Wilcox was about to charge the door, there came a sound from the inside. Hunter reached out an arm, barring Wilcox from his mad attempt to break the door down, just as the lock disengaged and the door swung open.

He'd expected to see the portly woman with the cropped hair. Instead, standing there was a smaller version of her—well, minus the nose ring and all the tattoos. It was a chubby, sleepy looking boy, probably no more than twelve.

He rubbed his eyes as he took them in, uninterested. "I was sleeping," he muttered.

Wilcox did not soften for the kid. "We're looking for Shilah Summerhill."

He sniffled. "Okay . . ."

"Do you know where she is?" he asked, growing increasingly impatient.

He shrugged. "How am I supposed to know? I told you, I was sleeping." He picked some sleep from his eye, inspected it, then flicked it toward them. "What are you guys, her probation officers again? How many times are you going to come here?"

Wilcox reached into his pocket, pulled out his credentials, and flipped them. The kid didn't look interested. "Who are you?"

"I'm Rocky. Her son."

"We want to talk to her. Can you call her?"

"Can't. Don't have a phone." He glanced past them. "Her truck's gone. Guess she went to work."

Wilcox asked. "How old are you?"

"I'm twelve. Almost thirteen."

"And she usually leaves you alone, without a method of calling her, when she goes off to work?"

"I did have a way of calling her, but I stepped on my phone and it's busted."

"I see," Wilcox said, taking out his own phone. "Where does she work?"

"Some warehouse downtown. I forget."

"If I give you my phone, can you call her?"

He shook his head. "I don't know the number. Wait, what are you? Some kind of child services people? She didn't leave me all alone. I *do* have a babysitter. At least, I think she is. But um, she's not here, either. She'll be back soon."

"And what is the name of your babysitter?"

He shrugged. "I forgot. I just met her yesterday. And I was kind of busy."

David's eyes narrowed as his heart jumped into his throat. "Uh, this babysitter . . . what did she look like?"

"I don't know. Old. Dark hair. Old." He shrugged.

Nice, vague description, kid, Hunter thought. As vague as it was, it could've been Mia. She showed up yesterday? It was a definite possibility. He looked around. If she was here, and she'd seen them, Mia would likely be on the run again.

While he scanned his surroundings outside for Mia, Wilcox was more interested in what was *inside* the trailer. "She live here with you?"

The chipmunk-cheeked kid nodded.

"Can we come in and take a look around?"

The kid crossed his arms. "Don't you need a warrant for that, guys?"

Hunter smiled. The kid had probably gotten it off of some television show, but he was right. Wilcox grunted. "Fine. We'll be back."

The kid slammed the door in their faces before they could even turn around.

Before they made it down the stairs, Hunter said, "So what, are you going to go back to headquarters and get that warrant?"

He shook his head. “No. Waste of time.”

“Because it would take too long?”

“No,” he said, climbing into his car. “Because it’ll create a paper trail. And we don’t want that.”

David slipped into the seat next to the Marshal and stared at him, surprised. No, they didn’t want that, if they were planning to find and question Mia North off the record. But it was the first sign Kane Wilcox had given him that maybe he was being a man of his word, and wouldn’t attempt to bring Mia in.

“So what do we do, now?” David asked as Wilcox started up his car and turned on the radio to some bland news station. He pulled out his phone and started to jab something in.

“It shouldn’t be too hard to find Shilah’s workplace. Yeah . . . here it is. I think we’ll need to go down there and pay her a visit.”

Hunter nodded in agreement as a newscaster said, “. . .murder out of Gun Springs City.” Hunter turned up the volume and listened as the speaker said something about a trailer park.

“Isn’t that where we are right now?”

Wilcox listened as the reporter went on, speaking about a victim who’d been stabbed multiple times. The killer was still on the loose and they were asking for the public’s help in finding who’d done it. “Yeah . . . sounds like a different park, though.”

“Sounds like almost an exact copycat of the murder that happened to Shilah Summerhill’s sister, doesn’t it?” he pointed out.

“Yeah,” he said, shifting into reverse and pulling out so that a cloud of dust enveloped them. “And if Mia did come here to help her friend find out what happened to her sister, then that’s the first place she’d look. Similar crimes.”

It made sense. “So we going there, first?”

Kane nodded and drove at an almost unsafe speed along the rutted roads, so fast that Hunter had to grab the arm rest to keep his head from bumping against the SUV’s ceiling. “Let’s go see if Mia North had the same hunch we just did.”

CHAPTER TWENTY

Mia sat in the passenger's seat of Shilah's truck, parked behind a tree, watching from a safe distance as the police raided the newest crime scene.

Shilah had been right. The Gun Springs City Trailer Park was smaller than Cedar Arms. But that was really where the differences ended. The place was almost exactly the same, with run-down trailers, covered in dirt, dents, and graffiti, and similar, suspicious residents who glared rather than waved.

"I know this place pretty well," Shilah was saying as Mia watched the police funnel in and out of a beige-colored trailer. "I used to run a cleaning business before I got arrested, to make money on the side. The woman who worked in the office used to hire me to straighten up in there, every two weeks."

"Did Merry know this place?"

Shilah shook her head. "I guess that's the real question. Not that I know of. Maybe. Like I said, who knows what she was up to while I was in the pen."

Mia sighed. The ambulance with the body had taken off, right when Shilah and Mia had arrived, and now the police were finishing with their clean-up investigation, packing up evidence and taping off the area with yellow crime scene tape. A few minutes before, there'd been crowds of people gathered about, phones up, trying to take video of the scene. But now that the body had been removed, the excitement was over, and they'd all pretty much gone.

"I wish I could get in there. If I could, maybe it'll tell me more about whether it was related to Merry's murder."

Shilah clapped her hands together. "I think we could arrange that."

Mia peered over at the woman. She didn't like that gleam in her eye. Whatever she was thinking was probably far too dangerous to attempt, under the circumstances. And yet, she really wanted to see what was in that trailer. "What are you thinking?"

"I could create a distraction, and give you some time to sneak in and check things out?"

"Distraction? Like what?"

She snorted. "I can think of something. You game?"

Of course, she was always up for any challenge. "Okay . . . but these guys won't stay around forever. Maybe we should just wait until they're gone?"

Even as she said the words, she felt her impatience growing. The two cops were sitting outside, joking and laughing about something, taking their time. They might be here all day.

Before Shilah could say anything else, Mia held up a hand. "Forget it. You're right. Let's do this."

"All right, I have an idea. Wait here." She got out of the car, went around back, and returned a few moments later. "Okay, ready. I'm going to drive up the path a little way, and you hide over there in those bushes."

Mia followed her pointed finger to some thick bushes, across from the front of the trailer. "Okay, and . . ."

"My rear tire is flat. Or at least, it will be. I'll pull up the road a little ways, stop, and play damsel in distress for a few minutes, while you get the goods."

Mia nodded and reached for the door handle. "Sounds like a plan."

She stepped out of the car, and keeping crouched, she quickly crossed the dirt road, following along a chain-link fence until she got to a line of honeysuckle bushes. She slid between the fence and the bushes, finding a place where she could easily watch what was going on through the branches. As she settled into a crouch, she watched as Shilah drove until she was just slightly behind the trailer, and saw her brake lights flicker on.

She came to a full stop, stepped out of her truck, and went to the back tire, which was now noticeably flat.

"Hey, boys!" she called over to the men who were laughing near their squad cars. "You think you can help me out over here?"

The men turned to look at her. "What's the problem?" one said.

"Flat tire. I don't know how to change them. My dear husband always did that for me, but he passed away . . ."

She was milking that sympathy card, because Mia knew her husband had split not long after Rocky was born, deciding he didn't want children a little too late in the game. Shilah hadn't missed him a single day; if there was one thing the woman didn't want, it was another husband. But even though it was quite the tall tale, it worked. The two young officers started to walk over. "You got a spare?"

"Maybe?" she said with a giggle, and the men exchanged glances and laughed, too.

As they all stared into the back of Shilah's truck, Mia slipped from the bushes and easily stepped across the shaded lawn, to the front of the trailer. Lifting the crime scene tape, she ducked underneath, rushed up the stairs, and hurried through the half-open door.

Inside, she found a regular bachelor pad, with nothing for décor except a few pizza boxes, some beer bottles in the sink, and an ashtray, full of cigarette butts. She held back a sneeze as she stepped in; the place could've used a good dusting. As she looked around, she heard a soft mewl, and saw a cat, in a cage, ready to be toted out.

"Aw, poor baby," she whispered, wishing she could crouch and give him a pet. But she had more important things on her mind now. She scanned the packaged things beside the cat and noticed a box full of drugs.

Well, that was one similarity, maybe, to Merry's killing. Maybe this was all about drugs.

But Mia felt like there was more to it than that. Mick had been Merry's provider, and Mia had cleared him. Dealers were pretty territorial, which meant that if he provided drugs to Cedar Arms, he was probably the only one. Unless Merry had another provider nobody knew about, it probably had nothing to do with the drugs.

The news reports said this latest victim, now identified as a Calvin Shoemaker, twenty-eight, single, was killed late at night. So that meant, more than likely, he'd been in his bedroom.

She turned to head down the hallway when she saw it.

The blood, right there, in the middle of the hallway. So he hadn't been killed in his bedroom.

In fact, he'd been killed in almost exactly the same spot in his house that Merry had been killed in hers, in the doorway, right in front of the bedroom.

That was interesting.

The blood was everywhere, pooling on the floor, smeared on the walls. It gave her flashbacks to the crime scene at Merry's. She carefully stepped past and looked into the single bedroom at the end of the hall, looking for an open window that the killer might've climbed through. There wasn't one. They were all shut, with shades pulled over them.

She spun. Even if the killer hadn't come in through the bedroom window, she felt sure that whoever it was had gained access to the house while the victim was unaware, and that the victim had been surprised to find them in the house.

And so yes, it really did look like it might've been the work of the same person.

"Thank you boys!" a voice blared from outside. It sounded close, like it was coming from the road on the side of the trailer. "Really couldn't have done it without you."

It was Shilah's voice, strained and strange.

It was a warning. Her way of telling Mia to get the hell out.

She jumped over the bloody spot where the latest victim had been killed and raced toward the door to the trailer. As she got there, she heard the two officers, laughing with one another. It sounded like they were right outside.

Frantic, her eyes darted around, searching out a possible hiding place. No, not a hiding place. She needed to escape. She needed to get as far away from here as possible.

Remembering the windows in the bedroom, she ran toward it, hurdling over the bloody spot and closing the door behind her. Calculating the window at the back of the trailer she'd have the best chance of getting out of, because there was a small bookcase underneath it, she climbed it, then slid open the storm cover and pushed out the screen. As she hoisted herself up, she heard the officers.

They were inside now.

She had to wiggle her way through the window, head first, like a worm. When she got through, she hoped for a soft landing, but the only thing there was a prickly bush. She fell on it, the branches scraping the skin of her cheeks as she tumbled to the ground.

When she sat up, she was prepared to break into a run. She scampered to her feet but only made it a few steps before a voice said, "Where are you going?"

Her heart froze in her chest.

She thought for sure she'd been caught, that she'd look up and find the two officers, handcuffs and guns at the ready. She pushed the hair out of her face, heart beating like mad as she tried to assess the danger. But she couldn't tell. The sunlight slashed down, straight into her eyes, so she had to shield her eyes from it in order to see the form in front of her.

It wasn't the cops. It was an old man, sitting in a beach chair in front of the trailer backing up to Cal's. He wasn't smiling, and yet there was amusement on his white-whiskered face.

She stood up, wiping the dust from her shorts and her legs, and moved away from the trailer, so that if the police came near, she could pretend she hadn't just jumped from its bedroom window. Gulping air to help her breathing return to normal, she walked over to him, hands on hips. "I'm—"

"An intruder. Got it." Now that she was closer, she could see his blue eyes. They twinkled.

"No, I'm—"

"People who aren't intruders usually use the front door."

She sighed and looked back at the trailer. "Yes, well, Cal and I were friends, and I left something there, but the police—"

"You another addict, like them?" He leaned forward, taking her in. "You don't look like an addict."

She shook her head. "Why, is he—"

"He deals. At least, I'm ninety-nine percent sure he did. I saw the weirdest types coming around his place, at all hours of the night. When he wasn't partying, he was dealing with a revolving door of guests, all wanting a piece of his stash."

Mia turned and peered over at the trailer. The police hadn't come out, looking for her, so it was possible she'd made a clean getaway. "A drug dealer, really?"

"Oh, yeah. Bet that was what did him in."

"You think it was a drug deal gone wrong, then?"

"Maybe. Makes sense. I was in there. Saw his stash. Heroin, I think."

"So you were friends?"

He snorted and patted his hands on his fleshy, jean-covered thighs. "Not likely. I called him trash. He told me to butt out of his life. So we weren't exactly neighborly. I don't even know why I bothered to call the police when I found his body. I should've just let him rot."

"*You* found his body?"

"That's right, I did. Found him lying right there in the hallway, bleeding his heart out." He seemed proud of the fact, and maybe even a little happy that his neighbor was dead. "Of course, you must've seen the crime scene, too, huh?"

"Well, I—"

"Don't know why you'd want to look at that." He shuddered. "I been in Vietnam, right on the Ho Chi Minh Trail, where I lost half my company before they pulled me out. I thought I was used to seeing things like that," he said, reaching down and lifting up his jeans to reveal a prosthetic calf, cut right below the knee. "But I don't like it. Not one bit."

"Yeah, I understand. But I was just—"

"Can't get around so good anymore. Got a heart problem, too. If I'd known that was what I'd see, I wouldn't have gotten up from bed. Didn't sleep well last night, after that."

"What *did* get you up from bed?"

"Well, it was like three in the morning. I heard him screaming bloody murder. Got up and looked out the window and saw him walking around his trailer, holding a baseball bat, calling after someone. Looking for someone. He looked angry. A little scared, too. Guess whoever it was must've stiffed him."

"He was walking around the trailer in the middle of the night with a bat?" she asked, interested. "Did you talk to him?"

He shook his head. "I might've muttered something about him being nuisance to this neighborhood, but he probably didn't hear it. I went back to bed, but when I did, I thought I heard a noise. It sounded like a scream. I tried to go to sleep but then curiosity got the better of me. Went round his trailer and found the door wide open, and him bleeding to death inside. So I went back to my place and called the authorities. By the time they came, he was already dead." He shrugged and poked his leg. "I was too slow."

"Don't beat yourself up. I'm sure you did everything you could," she said to him. "And by selling drugs, I think he was inviting that kind of trouble into his life. Did you happen to see anyone nearby when you were near his trailer?"

He shook his head. "No one."

"Do you know of anyone else who he might have had a grudge against him?"

"Like I said, he had a revolving door. I guess any one of them could've done it, but I don't know their names, or what they look like.

After a while, they all started to blur together. And I stay out of that business as much as I can."

"All right, thank you," she said as she heard a car door slam.

She went out around the trailer and looked down the road toward the park's exit. The police were driving away. *Of course, so that means that our little diversion was a waste of time.*

Mia was determined not to make this a waste of time, though. Both victims had been caught unaware and stabbed in their homes. Both victims were involved in drugs. That felt like too many similarities for it to just be a coincidence. So she was going to interview every person in this park, and find some connection to Merry's murder, even if she put herself in harm's way in the process.

CHAPTER TWENTY ONE

As Mia walked along the main road, trying to decide who to speak to first, Shilah pulled up behind her in the pick-up with the new spare tire on it. "Hey, stranger. Need a ride?"

Mia was so deep in thought that she barely heard her. She was thinking about Cal Shoemaker, walking around his trailer in the dead of night, with a baseball bat. If he'd had control over the situation, if it had just been a regular client who hadn't paid, would he have been doing that? It sounded like someone had spooked him, and he was afraid.

She'd gotten the same feeling, too, about Merry. Shilah had said she was clutching her gun, and probably scared about an intruder.

Yet another thing that tied these two murders together.

But that was all supposition. Really, she didn't know, and not being the first on the scene as an investigator put her at a serious disadvantage.

Shilah snapped her fingers. "Hello?"

"Hi," she said, startling out of her trance. "Sorry, what did you say? I was just thinking about something."

"I said, whew, that was a close one." As she got into the truck, Shilah turned down the radio and said, "What happened? Did you see anything interesting?"

"Not really. Except that he was murdered in almost the exact spot that Merry was, in the hallway outside his bedroom. What was more interesting was what his neighbor who found him said."

"And what was that?"

"That the victim had been running around his house with a baseball bat shortly before he was killed. It sounds like he was spooked, like Merry, with her gun."

Shilah's lips pulled into a tight O. "That's interesting. So you think there is a tie."

"Could be. I think we need to ask around and see if anyone else saw anything."

"Ask around . . . where?" Shilah's brow furrowed as they drove in front of Cal's trailer.

The two trailers facing his, on the other side of the street, were possibilities, but Mia understood Shilah's reluctance. There was a man sitting on the stoop of the house closest, cleaning a rather large hunting rifle, murder in his eyes. There was a dead deer in the dirt, next to him.

She winced. What had they done to deserve a look like that? Just existing?

"Maybe we'll come back to him," Mia said as she pointed to the other home. There was a woman with big hair and a little tube dress, smoking a cigarette.

When they drove over to her and stopped, she glared at them as she stubbed out her cigarette. She grabbed her beer—was she drinking beer this early in the day?—gave them the finger, and turned to go inside.

"Wait!" Mia said, struggling to open up the door and follow her. She really didn't want to have to question the scary hunter.

Before she could step outside, though, Shilah put a hand on her wrist. "Hold up."

Mia turned back. "What's wrong?"

"You're not gonna get much from these people. They don't like to talk. But I know someone who does. And she happens to have a lot of information about the people who live here."

Mia stared at her, moments passing before it finally dawned on her. "The woman who works in the front office? The one you used to clean for? She'll talk to us?"

Shilah nodded and pressed on the gas. "Oh, yeah. Name's Kathy. She owes me for underpaying me a couple of weeks when she didn't have the money. And trust me, one thing she's good at? Gossip. She never shuts up."

"That sounds perfect," Mia said as they drove to the front office.

When they stopped in front, Shilah took the lead, walking confidently into the small trailer at the front of the neighborhood. This trailer had a large porch on it, but it was old, the wood rotten and in need a of a new paint job. Shilah pulled open the old screen door and shouted, "Yoo hoo! Kathy! It's your favorite person!"

Mia went in to find something that looked like a general store—stocked with aisles of groceries, candy, magazines, and fireworks displays for the 4th. There was a sign that said, *TODAY'S SUB SPECIAL—Turkey.* Mia had thought this was just the rental office, but Kathy clearly had a side-business, selling everything nobody wanted to go out of the neighborhood to get.

A small woman with a head full of red ringlets poked her head up from behind the counter. "Shy! Haven't seen you in ages, baby girl! What are you doing in this neck of the woods?"

"Oh, little of this, little of that. You know," Shilah grinned.

"Tootsie said you were in the pen. That true?"

Shilah's face fell. "Well, yeah. Tootsie would be right. They got me on forging some checks. Just a couple months. But I'm out now."

"Got myself a new cleaning lady," Kathy said, her tone becoming more serious. "Truthfully, she's not as good as you are, but I had to do something when you up and disappeared."

"Yeah, sorry, I didn't get a chance to call in sick when I got hauled off to prison," Shilah said with a shrug, looking over at Mia. "Hey, Kath. Let me introduce you to. . ."

"Sue," Mia said quickly, glancing at Shilah. "Hi. I'm her cousin from out west."

"Oh, hey, girl," Kathy said, leaning far over the counter to give her a good once-over. "You visiting? That's nice. From where? California?"

Mia nodded. "Yep."

"Anyway," Shilah said, leaning in and looking around the place in a casual way. "What's new around here? Anything? We just heard you had a little excitement, on the news."

Kathy nodded, her face becoming serious to match her tone. "Oh, yes. You heard about that? Guy's been murdered. Cal, his name was. Really, kind of a loser. We're probably better off without him." She leaned in and whispered, "He dealt drugs."

Mia said, "You think that's what got him killed?"

"Who knows? Guy like that, probably has a million ways he could die. He liked to live on the edge; it's no surprise to anyone when he falls off, am I right?" She shrugged. "Of course, I had to go over there and see for myself."

"What did you see?" Shilah asked.

She rolled her eyes. "Same old, same old. Everyone standing around, gawking as they brought the body out. That sort of thing."

"So what's the consensus? That one of his clients just decided to kill him and steal his drugs?" Shilah asked.

"Yeah. I think that about sums it up."

"You think it's someone who lives around here?" Shilah asked.

"Could be."

"You know everyone," Shilah said. "If you had to guess, who would it be?"

"I thought it was maybe the guy who lived across from him. That guy's psycho. Always into his guns. But then I heard Cal was stabbed. So who knows?"

"Weird," Mia said, not sure she bought that explanation. "The girl who was murdered in Cedar Arms was killed almost the same way, or so I hear."

Shilah nodded. "You heard about that one, didn't you?"

Kathy clapped her hands together. "Oh, did I? That's all we've been talking about for the last week. Things are getting curiouser and curiouser, I'd say."

"The victim was my sister," Shilah said solemnly.

Kathy's face crumpled. "Was it? Oh, dear! I didn't know. They said a woman, but I didn't pay attention to the name. Poor thing. People have been talking about it, you don't know what's true and what's not."

"We've just been trying to figure out what happened, to give our family a little peace. What are people saying about it?" Mia asked. She was fully aware that while most talk was crazy, there were kernels of truth in there.

"Oh, all these wild theories. Everything from aliens to gang activity." She threw up her hands. "I don't know anything about either of those, so I'm still sticking with my idea. Bo."

Mia raised an eyebrow. "Bo?"

She nodded. "The guy across the way. You probably haven't seen him, but trust me, he's a weird man. He's the scary one with the guns I mentioned earlier."

"We saw him," Shilah said. "We were just back there."

"Oh . . . was he one of Cal's customers?" Mia asked.

"No, I don't think so. He's not the drug-using type. More of the 'Keep your hands off my guns' type, if you know what I mean. Always muttering under his breath, getting pissed at people. Honestly, I've called the police on him once or twice. I figure if there's going to be a shooting anywhere around here, he'll be involved."

"But these people were stabbed."

Kathy wrinkled her nose. "That's a little odd. Still, I find it interesting because he has a trailer in Cedar Arms, too."

Mia blinked. "He does?"

She nodded. "Oh, yes. He's lived in both places."

Shilah's eyes narrowed. "Funny. I don't remember seeing him at Cedar Arms."

"Oh, he did. You probably don't know him because he stayed to himself, and usually went on long hunting trips. I didn't worry too much about him because he was only here once in a while, before. But when that girl died in Cedar Arms, we got him here, full-time." She leaned both elbows on the counter and grinned. "Now if that doesn't scream *I'm guilty*, I don't know what does! He's trying to get away from the murder. I wouldn't be surprised if he leaves here, now, too. Can't say I'd mind it, but he deserves to be in jail."

"And you said his name is Bo?" Mia asked, now very interested in the man living across the way. It was entirely possible that Cal and Bo had gotten into an altercation, and that was the reason Cal was chasing him around his trailer and screaming.

Kathy nodded.

Shilah said, "I don't know that Merry knew anyone like that. I can't imagine her having anything to do with him."

"There's a good possibility with a freak like that, all she had to do was look at him the wrong way, and it would tick him off," Kathy said matter-of-factly. "I remember him going off on a guy for parking in front of his trailer. He came to me, all pissed off, demanding I do something about it. He was always coming in here, making complaints. But I told him, time and time again, there wasn't anything I could do. Maybe he decided to take things into his own hands."

Mia sighed, thinking of it. It would be terrible for a young woman to lose her life over something as silly as a minor dispute between neighbors. But it was a definite possibility, and the best one they had right now. "Thanks for the information," she said, turning for the door.

Shilah had been grabbing a bag of chips. She handed the cash over to Kathy and followed Mia outside. "So are we going to go over there now?"

Mia nodded.

Shilah bit her lip. "Sorry, but can we think this over a little bit?"

"What do you mean?" she asked, getting into the truck.

"Well, if this man is known to go ballistic on people for parking on the wrong side of the street, you think it's a good idea to accuse him of murder?"

"I wasn't going to just run in there and accuse him of murder," she pointed out, but even so, Shilah did have a point. This man, Bo, was a loose cannon. In her old world, she might've waited a little bit and called in back-up. But she didn't have that luxury anymore.

She took a deep breath, thinking. There really was no other way. If she wanted to catch this guy, she'd have to take the chance and confront him.

"Drive me over there. It'll be fine. I'll take care of everything."

Shilah winced and started the car. "If you say so. It's your funeral. Maybe mine, too, depending on how crazy he's feeling today. But I trust you know what you're doing."

"I do. I'm not going to poke the bear," she assured her friend. "It'll be fine."

Now she was just repeating it to assure herself.

Shilah reversed out of the parking space. But the moment she shifted into drive, Mia looked up and saw a fairly nice, mid-sized SUV, pulling into the trailer park. An older man with white hair, vaguely familiar, was at the wheel, talking to a passenger. At first, she thought nothing of it, but then she saw the passenger.

And that person was definitely familiar.

It was David Hunter.

She ducked her head low, beneath the dashboard, and it came to her.

The other man was U.S. Marshal Kane Wilcox, who'd been on her tail almost from the very beginning.

Kane Wilcox, and David Hunter. Her partner. The man she'd trusted, was in a car with the man who wanted to see her put away. The image flashed in her mind, two opposites, suddenly thrust together.

What was Hunter doing? He'd betrayed her once before . . . and yet, she'd had to trust someone, so she'd put her trust in him. Had that been a mistake? Her mind cycled through scattered thought fragments, nothing making sense.

"What's going on?" Shilah asked, confused, letting the car idle.

"Just drive," Mia muttered, pressing her cheek down on the center armrest and squeezing her eyes closed. "And try not to call attention to yourself."

"Where . . . to that guy Bo's place?"

"No! Drive out of the park. Quick."

The truck surged forward, swerving out of the gates, tires squealing. She continued on for a few tense seconds before slowing. As she did, Mia poked her head up to find them alone on the road, surrounded by trees and, on one side, what looked like the chain-link fence surrounding the trailer park. She let out the breath she'd been holding.

"What is that all about?" Shilah asked.

Mia shuddered, still shell-shocked by the image of her own partner in league with the U.S. Marshals, and she shook her head. "I don't know. I think the men in that SUV are after me."

"They are? Oh, no, girl. What are you going to do?"

Her mind swam. That was the question. None of the options that presented themselves seemed like good ones.

"We should get the hell out of here . . ." She hesitated. The instinct to run, as fast and as far away as she could, was strong. But so was the one to get back there and solve this crime. This latest suspect looked like their man, and she wasn't about to let him go so easily. "Maybe."

"Maybe?"

She sighed. She'd never been good with letting a criminal go, not when she could do something about it. But she couldn't take chances now. She nodded. "Yeah. I can't be here anymore. I'll get you in trouble. We need to go back to Cedar Arms. I'll gather up my things and go so that you'll be safe—"

"Hell no," Shilah said, wrapping her fingers tight around the steering wheel. "You've helped me so much already. I'm not about to let you just run off on your own. I'm helping you, with whatever you need. Just tell me what you need."

Mia gnawed on her lip. "Well, I guess I could—"

She froze as she heard the sound of an approaching car on the road.

"Shit," she whispered, watching the car appear in the rear-view mirror. At first, she saw that red SUV, the same one that had held the Marshal and her former partner. Frantic, she looked around, wondering if she should make a break for it. She held her breath and wrapped her clammy fingers around the door handle.

But then, as it drew closer, she recognized the front bumper. It wasn't that modern SUV. It was an older-model pick-up, similar to the one they were currently in. Even closer, and she recognized the man behind the steering wheel.

As he whizzed past them at a speed far exceeding the limit, she caught a look on his face. Hunched over the steering wheel, he looked angry. . . and a little desperate.

It was Bo.

Her heart kicked and she sat straight up, pointing. “Shilah! Follow that truck!”

CHAPTER TWENTY TWO

Kane Wilcox knew that David Hunter didn't fully trust him.

Personally, he didn't really care. If things went wrong, if he had even the slightest hint that Mia North was not the wrongfully-convicted victim that she's made herself out to be? He'd bring her in without a shred of guilt.

It didn't matter. No matter what, he was getting closer to his target. He could feel it. Mia had been at Cedar Arms. And if she wasn't here, at Gun Springs City Trailer Park, then she was somewhere close.

As they pulled in, David said, "This place looks like more of the same trash."

Wilcox swerved, narrowly missing a pick-up that was pulling out of a space near the office, as he took in the disrepair of his surroundings. It was rather trashy. On that fact, at least, he and David were in complete agreement. The trailer park had obviously seen better days. Most of the domiciles on the property looked like rusty rat traps. The people they passed looked not only suspicious, but hopeless, too, as if they were prisoners there. It gave Wilcox that same uneasy feeling he'd felt at Cedar Arms, and made him wish he could go back to his wife Dana, asap.

He pulled in front of the office, in the same place the pick-up had once been. When he cut the engine, Hunter said, "What are we doing here?"

"Going to talk to management and find out where the crime scene is."

He scanned the area. "Doesn't look as big as the other place. Bet we could just drive around and find it on our own."

Wilcox shook his head tightly. "Or we can be proactive and not waste time looking."

The FBI agent scowled at him, but said nothing. He simply followed Wilcox into the office. A middle-aged woman with red hair and too much cleavage was standing behind a counter, watching them guardedly. "What can I do you gentlemen for?" she said with little enthusiasm.

Wilcox flashed his credentials, getting about as much interest as he had from the Summerhill kid. He said, "You had a murder around here?"

She nodded. "I thought the police told me they were all done with it."

"We're not the police," he pointed out. "And we're not here for that. But we do have some questions about what happened. You know the victim?"

She shrugged. "Yeah. Not well, but I'll tell you what I told everyone else. He's a drug dealer. And I don't do drugs. I didn't really want his kind here, so I guess you could say I'm glad he's gone. But that doesn't mean I killed him."

"You know who did?"

She folded her arms over herself. "Why would the Marshals come out for a little murder in the middle of nowheresville? Oh, so you two must've made the same connection to the murder in Cedar Arms."

Wilcox lifted an eyebrow. "No, like we said, we're not here about the murder. But it's interesting you mention that. Did someone else make that connection?"

She frowned. "Maybe . . ." She tilted her head. "Why are you here?"

He pulled out his phone and opened it to a photograph of Shilah Summerhill. "We're looking for this woman. Have you seen her?"

Her face visibly blanched, but she shook her head. "Nope. I don't think so . . ."

"You sure?" Hunter said. "Look again."

"No. I don't know her. She doesn't live here. And what are you after her for, anyway? She commit a crime or something?"

"No, but she's traveling with a companion who did," Wilcox said, switching to the photograph of Mia. "How about her?"

The woman swallowed. "What did she do?"

"Murder."

Her eyes went wide. "Murder? Are you sure?"

"Yes ma'am, she's already been convicted and she escaped from federal prison. She's a danger to society, so if you have any information, I'd urge you to give it to us, now."

She sighed. "All right. She was here. Just a few minutes ago."

Wilcox couldn't fight the smile that broke out on his face. He was so close. Yes, he'd been close before, but now he felt like he could reach out and grab her. "Did she tell you why she was here, by chance?"

"Yes. It was about the murder of our resident."

"And let me guess," Hunter said. "She was the one who mentioned something about a connection between the murders."

She nodded. "I didn't know she was a wanted criminal. Murder! She doesn't look like a murderer," she said, clearly feeling the weight of guilt as she wrung her hands. "How was I to know?"

"It's not your fault," Wilcox said dismissively. He didn't care. What he did care about was the fact that the woman was close, and if he wanted to bring her in, time was of the essence. "So they were here about the murder. Did they go back to check out the scene of the crime?"

She shook her head. "Actually, they were past that. I think they'd already been there."

He let out a groan. Shit. That meant she was probably gone. Hell, she was probably in that blue pick-up they'd passed. And now, that old truck was probably on its way to God-knows-where. He knew it was a long shot, but he had to ask anyway. "Any clue as to where they were headed?"

"Absolutely," she said to his surprise, pointing toward the back of the trailer park. "I told them about a man named Bo, who lived across the street from Cal Shoemaker, the man who was murdered. Bo is antisocial, into guns, and walks around muttering to himself all the time. He's gotten into a few violent altercations with people around the neighborhood in the past, including the deceased. Not only that, he has a place in Cedar Arms, too. I told them if anyone was guilty of the murders, it was probably him. So they said they'd check it out."

When he heard that news, that glorious, incredible news, Wilcox began taking steps toward the door. "Where does this guy live?"

"Two back. In the red trailer on Oak. You can't miss it."

The second she gave him the address, he glanced at Hunter and shot himself out the front door of the office as if launched from a cannon.

"Thanks for the info," he called, rushing to his SUV. David Hunter was close behind, but he didn't care if he wasn't.

Hell or high water, nothing was going to stop him from finally running down Mia North.

Wilcox had come to learn not to expect anything in this case. He'd come to find that whenever he had a lead, it wouldn't pan out as he'd hoped. But this time felt different. This time, it felt like he was breathing down her neck. That he finally had her within his grip.

So as he pressed on the gas and shot out of the parking space, he'd let his hope run wild. He was actually prepared, when Oak Lane finally came into view, to see the dark-haired, slight-framed woman, standing in front of the red trailer. He could see himself, lunging from his SUV and snapping cuffs on her, finally.

Unfortunately, that was not what he found.

First, the crime scene came into view, easily visible because of the yellow crime scene tape roping it off. The police were long gone, though. On the other side of the street, the red trailer came next, but it looked deserted. There was no pick-up truck parked in front of it, and the doors and windows were sealed up tight. As he took in the depressing scene, a sinking feeling hit him, one that he felt clear down to his toes. He climbed from his car, wondering if Mia had somehow seen him.

No, she'd probably been in that truck and seen David, her former partner, and realized something was up. Now, she was probably gone.

He clenched his hand into a fist and punched the front hood of his SUV as he came around to the front steps. He was so close. He'd almost had her.

As expected, when he knocked, no one answered.

"Damn," he hissed out under his breath. "Goddammit."

"Something bothering you gentlemen?" a voice called out from down the street.

Wilcox lifted his head toward the voice, dipping his sunglasses to take in the sight of a barrel-chested older man, limping toward them.

David Hunter said, "We're looking for the man who lives here. Do you know him? Bo . . ."

"Knox," the older man said as he limped closer. "Sure do. We get together to compare war stories now and then. He was in Iraq. Good guy. What's the problem?"

"We have reason to believe he may be connected to a local murder," Wilcox said, pointing across the street. "You see what happened there, Mr . . .?"

"Berensten," he said with a nod. "Yeah, I live on the other street. Elm Lane. My trailer backs up to Cal's. The kid was a drug dealer. Not my cup of tea. But I found his body. He'd been stabbed. You're thinking Bo did this?"

"It's a possibility," Wilcox said.

He shook his head. "You're barking up the wrong tree. Yeah, no one likes him because he don't talk much, but that's the PTSD. I understand him, I was in Vietnam myself. That's why we got along."

"Do you happen to know where he might've went?" Hunter asked.

"No," Berensten said, shrugging. He was wearing a too-tight army t-shirt, the chest and pits dotted with sweat. "He has a bunch of property in a few trailer parks around here, I know. Might've gone to the Cedar Creek one. He likes to go fishing there on the weekends."

"Cedar Creek?" Wilcox repeated, making a mental note. *Bo Knox, Cedar Creek.* If Mia suspected him, it was a possibility she'd gone there. "All right. Thanks. One other question."

"Shoot," the man said.

"You see two women around here lately? Maybe in a blue pick-up truck?"

"Yep," Berensten said without hesitation. "The thin one even broke into the murder scene. I caught her, trying to slip out a bedroom window while the police were out front. She was asking me about the murder here. I told her everything I knew, which wasn't much—that the guy had been walking around with a baseball bat, a few hours before I found him dead in the hallway."

The two agents traded glances.

Wilcox shook the man's hand and the two men climbed back into the SUV again. Wilcox plugged the Cedar Creek Trailer Park into his GPS and got an address. This one was closer to the lake, on the wilder, less-developed side. He'd heard of it before, from a past partner. It was popular with hunters and other outdoorsmen who liked to take advantage of the wildlife.

"You see," Hunter said to him as they drove out of the park, on to the next one. "That's what Mia's doing. She's trying to solve her friend's murder. She could be heading to Mexico, to escape people like you, but she's staying here. Sounds pretty selfless to me, don't you think?"

That was all he'd heard from David Hunter, about Mia North. She was a regular saint. But he wasn't sure whether to buy it, yet. She had a reason to stick around here that went beyond that—she couldn't very well prove her innocence from a beach in Mexico. So he was withholding final judgement until he met her, face to face.

"Or crazy," he muttered, and pressed on the gas.

CHAPTER TWENTY THREE

Mia leaned forward in the passenger's side of the truck as they tailed Bo in his pick-up through the middle of town.

"Stay on him," she warned as another car pulled between them.

But then the car in front turned off and they wound up right on Bo's rear bumper. From here, she could see him glancing nervously in the rear-view mirror.

Mia added, "But don't get too close."

"I got it," Shilah said, sounding mildly annoyed. "Would you rather drive?"

"No, you're doing great," she said, as the truck pulled to the right and made a quick turn. Shilah followed, hanging back slightly.

Mia clasped her hands together on her lap. This was it. She felt it. This man, Bo, was guilty, and he was running. He'd gotten spooked by all the people around, asking questions, and now he was fleeing.

"Stay back, a little more," she warned, her voice vibrating with anticipation as Bo once again lifted his chin to the side. "He keeps looking in the rear-view mirror. I think he's getting suspicious."

"I'm trying."

They were approaching a stoplight in the middle of turning red. "Stop at this light," she instructed, and Shilah followed. "We'll catch up later."

She kept an eye on him as he surged forward, and by the time the light turned green, he was still in their sights, stopped at a light ahead. After that, though, there were no more lights, and Shilah fell into a comfortable place, a few cars back.

She said, "You really think this man killed Merry?"

Mia shrugged.

"I wonder how she came across him. You never can tell these days," she said with a shake of her head. "That's what I keep telling Rocky. If someone's upset at you, apologize and move on. Especially around this state, with everyone packing heat. You don't know who'll pull a gun on you, for the stupidest things."

Mia said nothing.

"Everyone's so angry," she said sullenly. "No one cares about anyone else anymore. It's a sad thing."

Mia pointed as the old pick-up turned again.

"I got it, I got it," she said, making the turn.

They continued to follow him, out of town, past all the stoplights, where the speed limit rose to fifty and the tightly packed houses on either side of the road turned to trees and empty fields.

"Where the heck is he going?" she mumbled under her breath.

"I don't know," Mia said as a sign came into view. *Now Entering the Town of Cedar Creek. Hunt, Fish, Enjoy Wild Texas as it Should Be!!*

"Oh, I know this place," Shilah said. "We're on the other side of the lake. This is where all the outdoorsy people usually stay. It's not as built up as the west side."

Mia could see that well enough on her own. They passed another trailer park on the lake, but he didn't slow. They continued on, a safe distance from Bo, until without warning, his truck disappeared.

Mia squinted, trying to see it up ahead. "Wait . . . where did it go?"

Shilah slowed and looked around. "I don't know. He pull in somewhere?"

"There's nowhere to pull, except for . . ." There were residential driveways, all gravel and dirt, hidden by the brush, only visible because of their rickety mailboxes stationed at the side of the road. "Did he pull into one of these driveways?"

"There!" Shilah announced, slamming on the brakes and quickly pulling to the side of the road.

Sure enough, the truck had done a U-turn and was now parked in the distance, on the other side, half-covered by the brush. As Shilah pulled off the road, she saw Bo go to the back of his truck and lower the tailgate. Then he looked around suspiciously.

Luckily, Bo didn't see them—Shilah had pulled far enough off the road that they were now well-hidden. They watched as he hefted something large and unwieldy onto his shoulder. It was long, and wrapped in a blue plastic tarp.

"What do you suppose that is?" Shilah remarked as Bo grabbed a shovel with his free arm and pushed closed the tailgate with his elbow, then headed into the woods.

Mia didn't want to say for sure, but the answer seemed obvious. A body.

This man was about to bury a body.

But who'd been murdered? Had he killed another person? And why was he suddenly hiding bodies? Merry and Cal had just been left in the same place they'd been killed. It didn't make sense, and yet, all the signs were there—Bo was a cold-blooded killer. They needed to do something, before he killed again.

She waited a moment, then, motioning to Shilah, crossed the street and slowly crept into the woods after him.

She continued in, Shilah behind her, forging her own path until she caught sight of the man through the trees. He was wearing a canvas camo jacket, but the blue tarp around the thing on his shoulder stood out among the foliage. She was easily able to track him at a distance, as he tromped over a narrow gully and past more and more trees, into absolute wilderness.

Behind her, Shilah's breathing became hard and labored. "Wait," she whispered, out of breath.

Mia put her finger to her lips, then turned to continue on. A moment, later, bright sunlight filtered through the trees, and she found herself at a clearing. On the other side of the clearing, Bo stopped, threw the tarp-covered thing on the ground, planted the spade of the shovel into the hard earth, and began to dig.

"He's digging a grave!" Shilah had come up on Mia without her noticing, and whispered that in her ear.

"I see that," she whispered, but there was really no need to. Not only was the man was making a lot of noise, digging, but also appeared to be in his own world, mumbling incoherently to himself. His cheeks were red and there was a crazed look in his eyes.

"So what do we do?"

"Stay here," she whispered, and crept around the perimeter of the clearing, hunched over, using the long grass as cover.

The man was so busy digging that he didn't notice her, getting into position, directly behind him.

For the thousandth time since she'd escaped, she wished she had her sidearm. Lacking that, she took a deep breath and got into position, readying herself for the attack. The man was big, definitely, at least six feet, and hurtling her small frame at him wouldn't do much damage. She'd have to use the element of surprise to her advantage, and try to disarm him that way.

Using all the energy in her, she jumped out and threw herself on his back, attempting to knock him off balance and grab for his shovel.

It didn't work.

Though she landed on his back, he didn't completely lose his footing. He stumbled forward only slightly, but easily righted himself. Muttering what Mia made out to be, "What the hell?", he kept his hands wrapped around the shovel's handle and whirled on her, slashing at her with it. The metal spade whistled through the air, just inches from her face.

She, however, did lose her balance, falling onto her backside and elbows with a jarring thud that she felt in every one of her bones. As she scrambled to collect herself and stand, he lifted the shovel up over his head, preparing to deal her a final, devastating blow.

She held up her hands in a last-ditch effort to defend herself, and prepared to roll out of the way when his eyes suddenly softened from sheer anger to absolute devastation. The shovel trembled in his hands, and he slowly lowered it. "Who are you?"

"It doesn't matter who I am," she said, lowering her hands. "I want to know why you're out here, in the middle of nowhere, digging a grave."

He swallowed, then looked over at the shapeless lump under the tarp. "I didn't mean it. It was an accident," he said, his voice suddenly fragile.

"What happened?" Mia asked. "I want you to tell me everything."

"I was just driving," he said, his voice pained. "Going the speed limit, minding my own business. And then, out of nowhere . . ."

He smacked his hands together.

"Died right there, at the scene. Before I could even get out of the truck. There was nothing I could do."

Shilah stepped through the grass and went to the package, picking at the packing tape that sealed it closed. She winced, bracing herself as she lifted the last bit of tape and prepared to pull it back. "Crazy guy," she mumbled as she worked. "This is *not* normal behavior, dude."

"I'm sorry?" Mia said, confused. She'd already noted a few things that didn't line up with Bo and the murders. But this was really out of left field. "You hit the victim with your car? So it was an accident?"

He nodded, then fell to his knees, pressed his fists into his eyes, and began to sob.

"Mia," Shilah whispered, standing over the body.

Mia turned to look at it. All she saw was brown fur, matted in blood. "What is it?"

"Looks like a dog."

He continued weeping, long, loud, obnoxious sobs, his body shaking as he was wracked with them. "I didn't mean it! I don't know who it belonged to, it got no ID, but it was someone's pet! Someone's best friend. And I took it away from them."

He dropped his chin to his chest and his sobs grew louder. Mia exchanged a glance with Shilah, who simply shook her head in disbelief.

"Why—why would you go through all this trouble?" Mia said, her hopes deflating. Here she was, in the middle of nowhere, the Feds hot on her tail, ready to catch her prime suspect red-handed, and the guy was clearly a pacifist.

He moaned and sniffled as he looked at the dog. "I love animals."

"But you're a hunter," Shilah pointed out.

He nodded. "*Some* animals."

"This is great," Mia groaned, turning and stalking away. "Just great. We're back at square one."

Shilah followed, her footsteps heavy as she plodded to keep up with her. "So what are we going to do now?"

This time, she didn't know. She couldn't go back to Shilah's trailer park. It was too dangerous, knowing that the U.S. Marshal was in town. It was very likely he and David Hunter had already swarmed Shilah's place.

She had no choice but to run and admit her defeat.

"I'm sorry, Shilah," she said in a small voice. "But I have to go. I wanted to find her killer, but—"

"It's okay, girl," the woman said, patting her hand. "I know you did everything you could. I understand you have to look out for yourself. But I can't just let you go. Where will you go now?"

"I don't know." *And you'll be better off if you don't know, either.* "Can you drop me off at the bus station, and loan me a few dollars?"

Shilah nodded. "Of course."

It was nice to have someone who cared, now, when it felt like the whole world was against her. But even Shilah's help didn't stop that gnawing feeling inside her. While part of the FBI, she'd never let a case go cold, and had been responsible for closing dozens of cases that had been dismissed as unsolvable. She loved solving cases—it was what she was born to do. Running away like this wasn't in her nature.

But there was nothing else she could do.

CHAPTER TWENTY FOUR

Mia was silent as they drove into the downtown area.

Though she probably should've been keeping an eye out for any sign of that U.S. Marshal, since she knew he was near, she couldn't get the thought of her recent defeat out of her head.

If she'd been free, she'd have found the killer. Likely, the person responsible would already be in jail. She'd have had the resources and the time to look into this case properly.

But now, a killer would go free, all because she had to save her own ass.

It didn't seem fair, but there was nothing she could do.

"Don't worry about it," Shilah kept saying to her. "I know you did all you could."

But had she? Maybe there was something else she could've done. Maybe she shouldn't have slept. She'd wasted time, too, pursing that guy Bo when he clearly had nothing to do with the crimes. She could've done more, made different decisions . . .

"The bus depot is right up here," Shilah was saying. "Go through my purse. I think I have a little cash in there. You're welcome to all of it."

Mia felt even worse, taking even a single dollar from this hard-working woman's wallet. Listless, she reached down and pulled it up, finding a small change purse. From it, she pulled a few twenties, leaving the rest, because she didn't want to clean the woman out completely. That would likely be enough to get her out of town, maybe to the Mexican border.

"I'll pay you back. I promise."

Shilah waved her away. "I wish I could do more."

She tucked the money into her pocket. As she was placing the wallet back into her purse, Shilah sucked in a sharp breath.

"Oh, no."

Mia didn't like the sound of that. Startled, she looked around and spotted the problem in her rear-view mirror.

Flashing red and blue lights. A police car.

Just then, the police car's siren went off, high and grating.

Shilah pulled over slightly and whispered through gritted teeth, "Maybe he just wants to pass me."

That hope disappeared as the cruiser followed them to the shoulder of the road. Mia's heart pounded. Shilah gave her an apologetic look, rolled down the window, put her hands at ten and two, and pasted an accommodating smile on her face as the officer sauntered up to the driver's-side window.

"Hello ma'am," the young officer said, leaning in to look at the two of them. "You know why I pulled you over?"

"No," Shilah said innocently, giving him a smile. "Was I doing something wrong?"

"You could say that. Let me see your license and registration."

Shilah leaned over and grabbed them from the glove compartment, handing them to the man, who stepped back to his car. "This isn't good," she whispered.

Mia looked around for escape. She could make a run for it. But that would leave Shilah, looking guiltier than ever. No, her best hope was to sit back and wait, and hope that this storm blew over.

A moment later, she watched in the rear-view mirror as the police officer opened the door to his cruiser and stepped out, heading for them.

He handed Shilah her license and registration, as Mia braced herself for the litany of charges the officer was bound to throw at her. *Murder. Evading police. Trespassing. Tampering with evidence. All of the above.*

"I'm sorry, officer," Shilah said with genuine remorse. "It won't happen again. Whatever it is. I really do my best to obey the law."

But to Mia's surprise, the officer leaned in and smiled. "Oh, I could probably see it happening again. These things are tricky, you know," he said, writing something on his pad, ripping it off, and handing it to her. "That's a warning for a broken taillight. You promise me you'll get that fixed so I don't have to pull you over again?"

She stared at it and nodded. "Oh. Yes. Yes! I will get it fixed right away," she babbled, holding the warning like she was about to kiss it. "Thank you. Have a great day, sir."

"And one other thing," he said, dipping his sunglasses and making eye contact with Mia. She felt her blood pressure skyrocket. "That license of yours is about to expire next month. Don't forget to get it renewed, all right?"

"Oh, yes. Of course," Shilah said, her voice a squeak. "Thanks for the reminder. And I'm so sorry about the taillight. I didn't notice it was out."

"Yeah, no problem. And don't beat yourself up too much about the light. It's one of those things people never seem to notice, because they're not looking there," he said, banging a fist softly on her window. "You take care now, okay? Drive safe."

"I will," she gushed, and as the officer headed back to his car, she let out a long, relieved breath and looked at Mia.

"Onto the bus station," she said softly, pulling out onto the road again.

Mia didn't notice when they finally pulled up at the bus depot in the center of town. As large and imposing as the station was, full of people and buses arriving and departing, Mia barely saw any of it.

She was no longer wallowing in the guilt over not solving the crime. No, her thoughts had turned to the crime itself, and things she might've overlooked. Though she'd looked for other murders, she'd never had the time to canvas the neighborhood, looking for more witnesses to the two murders.

By the time they got to the depot, she was completely inside her head, too busy thinking about something that the officer had said. *And don't beat yourself up too much about the light. It's one of those things people never seem to notice, because they're not looking there.* It intermingled with something Shilah had said, when she first arrived: *People around here like to keep to themselves.*

It suddenly struck her, a thought so big she couldn't ignore it.

"We're here," Shilah said, rousing her only partially from her thoughts. "Are you okay?"

She turned to look at Shilah, the thought solidifying in her head. "I just had an idea."

"About where you're going next?"

"No, about Merry's murder."

Shilah pointed to the bus station. "But—"

"I know, I know. But wait. Hear me out. We looked into other murders reported in other trailer parks, because of Cal. But remember how you said that people like to keep to themselves?"

Shilah nodded.

"Well, what if there are other murders that happened, and haven't yet been reported?" she asked, drumming her hands excitedly on her thighs. "Maybe they were just missing, and yet no one knows they've actually been murdered."

Shilah frowned. "Okay, yeah, but girl, how would you find those people? If someone from a trailer keeps to themselves, people probably wouldn't even report them missing."

"Maybe not friends," she said, taking Shilah's phone from the cup holder. "But places of employment would definitely keep a record of that. And I could've sworn I saw something about that in one of the articles I read about Merry. Can you unlock your phone for me?"

She handed it to Shilah, who unlocked it, handing it back. "We're double-parked here."

"One minute." Mia navigated through, looking through the articles, and frowned. "I don't know where I saw it. I could've sworn one of the women interviewed about Merry's death said something about a person who had just disappeared from her work, leaving no notice. Damn. Where did I see it?"

Shilah let out a little gasp and grabbed Mia's wrist. "Wait."

Mia looked up.

"I wasn't thinking about it. We all just thought she quit. But my supervisor at the warehouse was pissed because she never called in, never showed up again. Just wrote her off the books." Shilah blinked. "This was a month ago, right when I started back."

"Do you remember her name?"

She nodded. "Andrea. Andrea . . . Simmons." She snapped her fingers. "I remember her because Merry used to sit for her kid, years ago, when she was a teenager. She lives in a trailer park. Walnut Hill, I think. I remember *that* because my super never shut up about it."

"Why?"

"Well, Walnut Hill's not like other parks. It's a little fancy. Right on the lake. So she liked rubbing her address in people's noses, as if that made her special. After she didn't show up for a few days, my super said Andrea was too hoity toity for them and didn't need the money."

Another trailer park, completely different than the first two. Maybe she was overthinking and this Andrea had just gone off on her own retirement and hadn't told anyone. But maybe there was something more to it.

She knew she couldn't leave until she found out.

"Where is it?" Mia asked, growing excited as she plugged it into the phone and brought up the route. It was twelve miles away, on the other side of town.

There was a good chance that the Marshal probably wouldn't think to look for her there. At least, she hoped.

She held the phone up to Shilah. "Can you drive us there?"

Without hesitation, Shilah threw her truck into Drive. "Yeah. Let's go check it out."

CHAPTER TWENTY FIVE

Mia was amazed by the time they got to Walnut Hill. It was so different from the other places she'd visited. It looked like an exclusive resort, with giant, well-kept trailers, a swimming pool, manicured lawns, and a white, lakefront beach. The clientele she saw as they drove in were wearing bathing suits and sunglasses, as if on vacation.

She tapped on the armrest as they pulled into the front office.

"You stay here. The last thing we need is to call more attention to you," Shilah said, getting out of the truck. "I'll ask them where Andrea's trailer is. I'll tell them I'm a former co-worker and I'm stopping by to say hello. Be right back."

Mia nodded and watched as a sprinkler watered an already lush, green patch of lawn, full of bright pink flowers. As she did, she thought about the last two murders. If Andrea's disappearance did have anything to do with the other murders, one thing was for sure . . . it probably didn't have anything to do with drugs or money, as she'd been suspecting. This place was far too different.

Now that she thought about it, it really was a long shot. It didn't seem to have anything to do with the other crimes.

She sighed, wondering if this was just another waste of time. Maybe she should've taken the chance and boarded that bus headed to who-knows-where. By staying here this long, she was endangering herself.

As she was sitting there, the hot sun beating down on her, she saw something gleaming across the lawn.

Squinting, she tried to focus on it, and realized it was glass. It moved in unpredictable ways, though, first to one side, and then to the other. Gradually, she made out the shape of a person, camped out among the branches of a tree, holding a pair of binoculars.

"That's weird," she murmured, following the person's line of sight. Whoever was in the tree wasn't simply bird watching. His sight was set on one of windows of a nearby trailer.

Mia opened up the door and went closer, dodging the drops of water coming from the sprinkler as she neared. She looked to the window, confirming her suspicions. The guy was a creep, stalking the people who lived there.

She walked closer. "Hey!" she shouted.

He startled and glanced at her, then dropped his binoculars on a cord around his neck and tried to scramble from the tree. He half-fell most of the way, landing in a heap at the roots of the tree, but a second later, he jumped to attention and began to race across the green.

She followed after him. He was surprisingly spry, though, and they were evenly matched. She couldn't gain on him, no matter how hard she pushed. He zig-zagged through the line of trailers, trying to lose her, but she kept at him, never losing him. She saw him rush up the steps to a silver bullet Airstream trailer, throw open the door, fling himself inside, and slam it with a thump.

Rushing up to it, she banged on the door. "Let me in. What the hell were you doing, spying on people?"

No answer.

She banged again. "I know you're in there. Don't make me break this door down."

The man didn't answer. She kept banging, first with her hand, then with her fist.

"All right, you asked for it," she called. "I'm coming in on one, two—"

The door flew open and a young-faced, yet balding man stuck his head out. He was holding his phone. "Leave me alone. I'll call the pol—"

She muscled her way in, easily grabbing the phone from him. When he lunged for it, she elbowed him in the chest, forcing him to stagger back, breathless, and fall into an overstuffed couch, part of a matching set. "You were spying on your neighbors. What the hell was that all about?"

He held his chest, panting, but said nothing.

She looked around the place. It was white and spotless, with modern furniture and fixtures. Whoever this man was, he was making a good living. "Are you going to answer for yourself?" she demanded.

He shrugged. "I have nothing to say to you. I didn't do anything wrong."

She stalked across the living room to his workspace—a large drafter's desk in a cubby in the corner of the room. Hanging over it was a giant map, with different locales circled. "So you think spying on your neighbors is nothing wrong?" she mumbled, trying to make sense of the map in front of her.

"I think you're the one trespassing," he snapped at her. "This is outrageous!"

He was right; if he had managed to call the police before he opened the door, and they were on their way now, she'd be in huge trouble. But though that possibility tickled the back of her mind, the pieces of the map suddenly came together, making sense.

The lake was in the center of the map, and all around it, circled in yellow, were different trailer parks. Four different trailer parks, to be exact, among them—Walnut Hill, Cedar Arms, and Gun Springs City Trailer Park.

Two confirmed murder sites, one possible murder site, and the other . . .?

She whirled on him. "What does this mean?"

He shrugged. "Nothing. I just like to look at maps."

"And you like to stalk people, too. You go around looking at them when they don't know they're being watched. That's really creepy. And then, what do you do?"

He frowned. "What do you mean, what do I do? Nothing. And I'm not being creepy. I just like watching people from all walks of life. Seeing what they do. It's people watching. Nothing wrong with that."

"You were looking into someone's house. That's the problem," she said, holding his phone in her fist. "What were you going to do? Is that what you did in Cedar Arms? In Gun City? Right before you killed those people?"

"What?" he responded at once. "Lady, you're crazy."

Mia's eyes flickered to the desk. Her eyes widened as she saw them, lined up on a piece of cheesecloth, where any normal person would have a laptop.

Knives. Great, big, wooden-handled hunting knives, of various sizes.

"What are those for?" she asked, hardly able to take her eyes off them.

He gulped loudly. "I carve. I'm a carver. You know, I like to whittle. It's my hobby."

The words registered only lightly in her head. His hobby. It didn't make sense. If it was his hobby, where were the wood shavings? Pieces of bark? His finished creations? She didn't see them anywhere. *Liar.*

No. Worse than that. *Murderer.*

He'd killed them. Cal. Merry. And who knew who else? She'd found him.

She started to turn toward him. "You don't expect me to—"

Without warning, he lunged at her, his hands gripping tightly to her shoulders. She stumbled back, the backs of her thighs hitting the desk. His eyes were wild and unfocused, spittle flying from his mouth as he snarled, "You! *You*!"

He moved his hands up in effort to wrap them around her neck, to choke her. Still shocked by the attack, she reached behind her, fumbling aimlessly for one of the knives. Her fingertips touched a blade, but she registered no pain. There was too much adrenaline coursing through her veins. Finally wrapping her hand around the wooden handle, she brought it around and sliced at him.

He backed up at once. "You bitch! What do you think you're doing? Trespassing in here and stealing my tools?"

She waved the knife in front of him. He stopped at once and held up his hands in surrender, still huffing in rage. "Why did you kill them?"

His face twisted. "I told you, I have no idea what you're talking about. That map? It's a list of places I've been to. I like to move around. That's all. This is America, isn't it? I'm free to move around? I don't deserve to be treated like this." He started to advance on her again. "This is my house, and I'm a law-abiding—"

"Get back," she shouted at him, trying to devise her next move. In ordinary circumstances, this was when she'd call in back-up, and the police would flood in. She didn't have that now. When the police came, she had to be gone.

Shilah.

She inched toward the nearest window and peered out, trying to spot Shilah's truck. But the window looked out upon another trailer.

She felt a sudden pressure on her wrist and turned to find the man, grabbing for it. She shoved him off, pressing him up against the kitchen counter and bringing the blade up close to his throat. "Don't do that again."

"I'll scream."

"You do that, and I'll slit your throat," she said, spotting a coil of duct tape on the counter. She grabbed it with one hand, bit off a piece to start it, and pulled a long length of tape. "You're going to sit right here and wait for the police to come. Do you understand?"

His eyes widened. “What are you doing?”
“Making sure you don’t get away this time.”

CHAPTER TWENTY SIX

"You're going to pay for this!" the man said as Mia duct-taped him to a chair in the kitchen. "You're gonna—"

She stuffed a sock in his mouth and tied a cloth around the back of his balding head, sick of hearing him grumbling. "Now you're just going to have to sit here and wait. Calm down."

She reached into the back pocket of his khaki shorts and pulled out a wallet. Opening it, she found his driver's license. His name was Joseph Draven. From an address in Winter Park, Florida. She wondered when he'd come up this way, and how long he'd been here. Had he had other victims?

Well, it wasn't her problem, now. She'd have to leave it for the police to figure out.

She'd never been one to go after the glory that came with solving cases, but there was some satisfaction that went along with a job well done. She didn't feel it, now. Maybe it was because it didn't feel complete unless she was the one snapping the cuffs on and toting him to jail.

But that couldn't be helped.

Giving the killer one last look, she stepped out the door and closed it behind her. Then she took note of the road the Airstream trailer was parked on—Lover's Lane.

Jogging back to the front of the development, she found Shilah standing there, outside her truck, looking confused. "Oh, there you are!" she said when she spotted her. "Where were you?"

"I found him," she said, smiling proudly.

"You found her? Good! Is she all right?" Shilah said with a sigh of relief. "Because the lady in that office wouldn't tell me anything. I asked her if she knew where Andrea was, and she told me—"

"No, this has nothing to do with Andrea," Mia said. "I found him. The killer."

Shilah stood still in her obvious confusion for at least ten seconds. "What? Wait. What did you just say?"

“I found the killer. His name is Joseph Draven and he lives in the Airstream on Lover’s Lane.”

Shilah’s voice rose an octave in her excitement. “What? How do you know?”

Mia recounted the story of how she saw him in a tree, spying on his neighbors, and followed him back to the house. “He wasn’t just a little off. He clearly had a few screws loose. Not only that, but he had a map with the two trailer parks outlined, and a collection of knives.”

Shilah’s covered her mouth, which was now in the shape of an O. “And did he tell you why he killed her? Was he stalking her?”

“He didn’t tell me,” she said, reaching into the truck and grabbing a napkin and a pen from the center console. She started to write. “I need you to do something for me. When I’m gone, I need you to call the police and tell them where to find him, and also, ask them to look into Andrea and tell them you think she might be another one of his victims. Can you do that?”

“Yes, but . . .” Shilah didn’t take the paper when Mia held it out to her. “What are you going to do?”

She wasn’t sure about that. The plan was to get away from this area, since the Marshal was after her. But whether she hitched a ride or took a bus was still up in the air.

“I’ll figure it out.”

She stared at the paper hanging between them for a beat, and then took it. Then, unexpectedly, she leaned forward and pulled Mia into a hug. When she pulled back, Mia saw tears in the woman’s eyes. “Thank you. I can’t tell you how much this means to me.”

“Look. I’m not sure it’s over yet. Yes, he’s probably the killer. He’s definitely a creep, and he has the weapons and has been at the same parks. But that’s all we have right now. Someone needs to test the material at Draven’s house and see if the DNA matches up to the crime scenes, and I can’t do that. The police need to, so they’ll have to take it from here. Which means I have to make myself scarce. Okay?”

Shilah pressed her lips together. “He’s our man. I can feel it. You really tied him up and left him in his trailer?”

Mia wasn’t so sure. She didn’t know if it was actual doubt causing her uneasiness, or the fact that she couldn’t see this through to the end. “Yes. You’ll have to tell them you did it; I don’t want to give them any hint that I was involved. Joseph might say something about me, but if the police ask questions, just deny it. The police should be able to follow the breadcrumbs and find out if he's really our man. I've got to go."

"Now?"

She stuck her hand into her pocket, feeling for the money. Hopefully, that would get her far enough. She nodded. "It's better if I'm nowhere near when the police come."

"But where—"

"Trust me. It's better if you don't know."

Shilah took the paper, ripped it in half, and grabbed the pen, scribbling something down. "My cell number. In case you need me. At any time." She hugged her again. "All right. Take care of yourself, Mia."

She smiled. "I will."

Turning toward the trailer park exit, she headed off, hoping to hitch a ride and be safely away before the police swarmed the place.

*

Mia sat up in bed in the Cozy Shack Motel, watching mindless reality television, eating fried chicken, and thinking about the case.

She'd made a plan as she walked the road with her thumb out, hoping someone would come along and pick her up. She'd get far away from this place, maybe go North this time, into Oklahoma. There was a chance her name wouldn't be posted all over the news there.

Unfortunately, no one had stopped.

Then, the rain came. It was not just rain but a complete downpour, soaking Mia to the skin. The rain was so heavy that she could barely see in front of her.

Eventually, she made it to a motel, where a family had been checking out, on their way home from vacation. The mother had felt guilty, given her their leftover dinner and money, and told her that they were booked into the motel for the rest of the week, and she was welcome to have their key. Since she had only the sixty dollars Shilah had given her, and it was late, cars heading north were scarce, and she had nowhere else to go, she took them up on the offer. She'd at least stay the night, regroup, and then try to find a way out, tomorrow.

Now, showered, towel on her head, letting her only clothes dry on a line in the bathroom, she shivered. As she nibbled on a drumstick, she wondered if stopping here, so close to the crime, was a mistake. The police would be going crazy, tonight, after finding Joseph Draven. They might not be looking for her, but that didn't change the fact that the U.S. Marshals were. And they were not far behind.

She tossed the remains of the drumstick into the bucket and sucked down a tepid soda, just as the reality show ended and switched to the eleven o'clock news.

A reporter stared into the audience, his face grave. "Tonight, a developing story out of Walnut Hill Trailer Park in Gun Springs City. A decomposed body was found in a trailer there, apparently the victim of murder. The trailer belonged to an Andrea Simmons, forty-five, who had been living in the park for the last year."

Mia set her empty drink cup down, grabbed the remote, and scooted to the edge of the bed and she jabbed the button to up the volume.

So Andrea was dead. So she had been a victim of Joseph Draven.

"The police were called to the scene of the crime by an unknown tipster who had also pointed the finger for the murder to another resident of the park. However, though the police investigated and questioned this individual, no arrests have been made."

She slapped both of her thighs. "What the hell? They cleared him?" she said aloud, wishing she could've been a fly on the wall during the questioning. "Why?"

The reporter continued. "It appears the victim had been stabbed, and in looking for a possible connection to two other stabbings in nearby trailer parks, the police found an interesting connection. A reporter is on the scene to give us the latest. Henry, what can you tell us?"

The feed then cut to a man, standing in the dark, in the rain, in front of the Airstream trailer. "Yes, thanks, Bob. It's a chaotic situation all around. Originally, the police thought that the murders in other trailer parks were drug-related. However, with the finding of victim Andrea Simmons, the police are now looking into other possible connections. It turns out that victim Cal Shoemaker had visited Andrea Simmons several times before she disappeared. So now the police are looking into all the recent stabbings, to see if there might be a common denominator here."

Mia stared at the television, goosebumps prickling the back of her neck.

Cal and Andrea Simmons knew each other. And Merry . . .

She recalled what Shilah had said. *Merry used to sit for her kid, years ago, when she was a teenager.*

There it was. The common denominator.

Mia rushed to the bathroom and fished the water-stained paper with Shilah's number out of her shorts, drying on the line. Back at her bedside, she grabbed the hotel phone and fumbled a bit, trying to figure out how to get a dial tone. Then she plugged in the number.

"Yeah?" Shilah's low voice said.

"Hey, it's me," Mia said quickly.

"Wow. I didn't think you'd be needing me this quick!" Shilah said with a laugh, clearly happy to hear from her. "Is everything okay?"

"Yeah . . . well . . . no. I need your help."

"That's what I'm here for," her friend said brightly. "Guess you heard that they didn't arrest that Draven guy. Something about not having evidence, and an alibi, and—"

"Yeah, I know. But I think I know who did it."

"Who?"

"You said Andrea Simmons had a kid, and Merry used to babysit for him?"

There was a pause. "Yeah. But jeez. That was a long time ago. Do you think he has something to do with it?"

"Yeah. Turns out Cal Shoemaker knew Andrea. I don't know how they're related, but they are. And Merry was her babysitter. So there's the connection. And I think this kid—who has to be an adult by now—might have something to do with it."

"Ah!" Shilah said. "Makes sense."

"Do you know anything about him? His name?"

"Logan. That's it. His name was Logan. Cutest little kid, from what I remember. He'd be, oh—twenty by now?"

"Right. About. Can you look him up? I don't have access to the internet, or else I would. See if there's an address or something?"

"Yep. Hold on tight, girl. Be right back."

There was a long pause, where Mia leaned back against the headboard, thinking. The police might be able to make the connection on their own. But how many people might die before they did? If she got the address, she could take a taxi there, confront the man, and put an end to this, tonight.

There was the sound of movement on the other end of the line. "Got it!" she said triumphantly. "He's still living with his dad, Keith

Simmons, in—get this. Another trailer park. Wild Texas. Fourteen Amber Road. We passed it earlier today on the way to Walnut Hill. Remember?"

She did, and if she was right, it wasn't far away. She could walk it. Even though her feet were sore from her failed hitchhiking attempt, and it was still raining, she would do it. Tonight.

"Thanks," Mia said quickly, preparing to end the call.

"Wait! You're not going over there now, are you?"

"I have to," she said, taking a deep breath. "We need to put an end to this."

"I'll meet you there."

"No, you won't," she said quickly. "I don't want to call attention to myself. It's better if I'm there on my own. And it could be dangerous. Promise me you'll stay home."

She sighed. "All right, as long as you know what you're doing. Call me if you hear anything. I want to know."

"Of course."

"And be careful," she added.

"I will." Mia hung up the phone and raced into the bathroom to get changed. Her clothes were still wet, and bound to get wetter, but she couldn't let that bother her. She had a killer to catch.

CHAPTER TWENTY SEVEN

Mia didn't have a GPS to track how long it would take to get to Wild Texas, but she knew, based on their travels earlier, that it was somewhere up the road. However, as she walked, she realized it was a lot farther than she'd expected. But the rain had dwindled to a light drizzle and the night was actually pleasant, so she made it there slightly before midnight.

As she stepped through the gates, a wooden split-rail fence with a picture of a smiling cowboy and the words WILD TEXAS RESORT! greeted her. Despite its name, the place was pretty dead, except for the beat of some rap music, playing far away. Unlike Cedar Arms, people weren't gathered together, having a party. As she walked in, there were a few streetlights at not-so-generous intervals, lighting up the street signs.

Amber Road was the first street she came to. She walked carefully down it, squinting in the moonlight to find the lot numbers. When she found fourteen, she expected to see it looking like all the others—dark.

But there was a light on, inside.

She looked up at the window, covered by a shade, then climbed the steps and knocked.

There was no answer.

When she knocked harder, the door gave way a little. She pressed it firmly and realized it was cracked open.

She pushed it all of the way and the first thing she saw was a light, in the corner of the living room, shining over a balding man, sleeping in a recliner.

"Hello?" she said, stepping in, but it was in that moment she realized something was wrong. The man's chin lolled too far into his chest, in an unnatural, lifeless way.

When she took another step in, she saw the blood, staining his white shirt.

She ran to him and knelt in front of him, feeling his hand.

He was dead. Stabbed. Logan Simmons's father, his skin cold. He'd been here a while.

But where was Logan?

Carefully, she turned, scanning the place. She went quietly into all the rooms, looking for him, but the house was empty. In the hallway, she stopped at a bedroom and turned on a light.

The room was draped with tapestries from bands Mia had never heard of—with Blood, Death, and Hell in their names. They were riddled with skulls and barbed wire. There was a giant computer screen set up in the corner, as well as a litany of war and shooting video games. It was the typical angry teenage boy's bedroom, and from the rumpled sheets and mess on the floor, it was clear no one picked up after him.

When she scanned his dresser, she saw it.

A photograph of him, and his father, in hunting camouflage, standing in front of a dead deer, their catch. The father was holding a rifle, but little Logan, probably not more than twelve or thirteen in the photo, was proudly holding a giant hunting knife.

Her eyes drifted down to piles of hunting magazines, to a postcard that said, *Kill Everybody.*

This guy had been harboring a lot of hate and resentment for a long time.

But he wasn't here, now.

She walked through the home, navigating to the front door, trying to find some clue as to where Logan Simmons might have fled to. But there was nothing.

She passed by the phone, on the kitchen counter, and picked up the receiver. Maybe this was all she could do. Call the police, leave an anonymous tip about the murdered man, and steal away, hoping they could find and apprehend Logan on her own.

No. She couldn't let it end like this. She had to find him, somehow.

But how? It was late. There was no sign of him. Maybe Shilah had some idea of other family members who might know where he is, or maybe the neighbors did, but it was too late at night. There was nothing she could do now.

She picked up the phone.

"All right," a gravelly voice called from outside. "Come on out with your hands up."

She stiffened, turning toward the door. Was that the police? She looked around for some method of escape, but she was trapped.

"I'm not getting any younger!" the voice said again. "Come out or I'll shoot."

That didn't sound like typical police lingo. She crept to the door and listened.

"I'm serious. You'd better have a good reason for trespassing in there."

Mia pulled open the door and put her hands up. She found an old man in slippers and a bathrobe, standing at the foot of the steps, a shotgun pointed straight at her.

He cocked the gun. "Who are you? You have a reason to be here?"

"I . . ." She looked around, trying to think of an excuse.

"I thought so. Trespassing. Well, me and Keith, we have a deal. We look out for each other's property when the other's gone, make sure no one tries to steal nothin'. I thought you were some of that delinquent son's buddies, trying to steal from him."

"I'm looking for the son. Uh, Logan," she said, not moving. "I'm one of his former teachers. And he sent a message to me. I'm worried he's in trouble."

The man snorted. "I'd say he's in trouble."

"Of what sort?"

"I looked in on the kid from time to time, but he's always been messed up. Never graduated. Spends all his days and nights locked in his bedroom, doing God-knows-what. Can't blame Keith. It was that mother of his."

His mother's dead, and has been, for nearly a month. Had he been keeping that a secret, all this time? "Do you know where he is?"

He nodded. "Keith was going down to Galveston for vacation," the man said. "He said he wasn't going to take Logan unless he cleaned up his act and showed that he was gonna get a job. But I guess the kid fouled up again because I haven't seen Keith. But I did see the boy earlier today. Couple hours ago, before dinnertime."

"Did he say where he was going?"

He shrugged. "I don't know. But he does have an uncle. Out on Summer Moon Street."

"Where?"

He motioned behind her. "Summer Moon. The orange trailer on the end. His uncle's younger, more of a friend than an uncle, if you know what I mean. A little bit of a drunk, though. But I know he usually goes over there sometimes to hang out with him and play video games."

"Great, thanks," she said, taking a step down.

"Wait, wait, wait," he said, shoving the gun in her face. "I didn't say you could go yet. What are you here for? What were you doing in there?"

She pulled the door closed behind her. "I told you, just checking on him. But he wasn't there."

His eyes narrowed. "How do I know you didn't steal nothing?"

She held up her hands. "I don't have anything, do I?"

"No, guess not." He lowered the gun.

"So may I go check on Logan at his uncle's house?" she asked.

He waved her off. "Yeah, whatever. Just go. And tell him if you find him that our little talk from earlier today isn't over."

She'd already taken the first steps toward the back of the park, but when she heard that, she stopped. "What was that about?"

"Oh, he's always terrorizing Poochie, my dog," he said, motioning to the trailer next door. "Taking his knife out and waving it at him, saying he was going to cut his heart out. So I told him that if he tried anything like that again, I was going to report him to the police." He snorted with great satisfaction in himself. "I told him to go get a job and stop being a lowlife."

Something inside her tightened at the thought. Saying something like that to a kid who was clearly as unhinged as Logan Simmons was a little like poking a grizzly bear. But he hadn't known. The neighbor had just seen a troubled kid. And there were plenty of troubled kids who'd never go on a murderous rampage.

She watched the man walk off, toward his trailer, opening the door as a tiny pup yipped at the man's ankles.

Terrorizing Poochie. With a knife.

Logan Simmons was more than just a troubled kid, now. He was completely unhinged.

Spinning, she ran as fast as she could toward Summer Moon Lane. She had to get to Logan's uncle before it was too late.

CHAPTER TWENTY EIGHT

Logan Simmons sat in the darkness at the back bedroom of the small trailer, staring at his one prized possession in the world, twisting it so that it would glisten in the minimal light.

It was his Williams May Skinner Knife, a beauty, given to him by his late grandfather.

It had been his pride and joy, ever since he'd started hunting with his grandfather, when he was a boy. Then, when his grandfather died, he'd had to go on hunting trips with his asshole father. Only once or twice a year, whenever his dad could make the time out of his busy schedule of screwing his secretary. Despite his father drinking too much and getting on his nerves about when he was going to stop playing video games and make something of himself, those trips out in the field, with the knife in his pocket, were some of his favorite memories.

He pushed it back into the leather holster, then took it out, savoring the slicing sound it made as he moved it around. The smell of fine-grain leather filled his nostrils, and he couldn't wait to replace that with another smell. The smell of blood.

He shifted in his hiding place, peering out of the back bedroom, looking at his next target as he walked from kitchen to living area, with a beer and a plate full of Doritos. Already drunk, he spilled a little of it on his way to his recliner, since his eyes were plastered on the television. Cursing, he just left it there, to seep into the matted carpet.

The fat pig never slept. All he did was eat. And eat. And drag his trash around the Earth, poisoning it. His stomach was like a beach ball, and he was probably suffering from a serious case of adult diabetes.

And people called Logan a waste of space? All his life, he'd been treated like he was nothing. But this guy? Here was a true waste of space. Never did anything good on this planet, his entire life.

And now his day had come.

His mother's day had come, about a month ago. Summer had just started, and though he was looking into getting a new job, none of the places he'd applied to had called him back. It wasn't his fault. So instead, he was planning to say, "To hell with it all," to kick back and have a relaxing summer. He'd get a job in the fall.

But then his mother had to go and run her mouth.

She was always harping on him. All the damn time. She wanted him to work. To dress better. To put away the video games. To help around the house. From the moment he woke to the moment he went to bed, it was just more of the same—blah, blah, blah, never shutting up.

She'd bitched at him for spending all his time in his room, without getting it through her fat head that *she* was the one who'd forced him in there.

So he'd snapped.

It was over something stupid. He could barely remember what. Orange juice. Or milk. She'd complained because he drank it all and left the empty carton in the fridge. *Why don't you get your lazy ass up and go to the store, Logan?* She'd complained to him. *I thought I'd raised you better but you're just like your dad!*

That was it. He got the knife from his dresser, came back, and dug it into her chest before she even knew what was happening.

Logan smiled at the thought of it, of the exhilaration he felt when he finally plunged the knife into his victim's middle. He loved the way their eyes would widen, the way they'd expel all the breath in their lungs, some of the last breaths they'd ever take. He loved that look on their face of utter surprise, as if to say, *Why, Logan? Of all the people in the world, I never expected this of you.*

They'd never expected anything from him at all. And that was their problem. Now, he was making it his business to make them see him in a whole new light.

Right before their eyes closed, forever.

The television was loud—the sounds of late-night television talk show—a television personality's voice followed by canned laughter. He didn't watch that shit. He liked his video games, and that was all. His father watched all that crap, his mother, too. That was probably the only thing they'd ever agreed on in their short, bitter marriage. That, and the fact that they probably never should've had kids.

Which was why he'd been left to fend for himself, most of the time. The only person who truly cared about him was his grandfather. And when he was gone, Logan was on his own.

He actually liked it that way. Over the years, he gradually learned that he'd rather be alone than with any of the so-called "caretakers". In fact, he'd rather be alone than with anyone else in the world. People disappointed him. They *always* disappointed him. His babysitter when he was a kid, who'd lock him in the bathroom while she went and shot up. His older cousin, who'd always treat him like trash. And so many more, throughout the years. He had a long list of them—disappointment after disappointment. Which was why he'd learned to only depend on one person—himself.

And now, he was gradually doing his part to wipe these useless lives from the face of the Earth, so they couldn't mess with anyone else.

The guy on television must've said something funny, because in the living room, the man snorted, then laughed so loud he started to choke. He caught his breath and pounded the arm rest of the recliner with his hand.

Logan could see all this from his spot, down the hallway. He saw when his stupid dog got up, heard his collar jingling and his toenails scraping on the tile floor as he plodded down the hallway.

Crouching, he opened the door a little more. "Here, doggie. Here you go. Come here, baby. Give me some love," he whispered, offering his hand to smell.

The dog sniffed it and leaned in for a pet, never making a sound. As far as guard dogs went, this one was totally useless. Logan stroked his long fur, feeling a sort of solidarity with it. *I bet people call you a waste of space, too.*

Straightening, he took a breath, his veins pulsing with the excitement as he lifted the knife and stepped past the dog. He couldn't wait.

It was time.

CHAPTER TWENTY NINE

Mia ran up to the orange trailer, sure that she'd come upon another bloody murder scene.

From the outside, it looked quiet, like everything was fine. Some of the lights were on, and though she could see shadows moving inside, she didn't hear any loud noises or signs of a struggle.

She climbed the steps as fast as she could and tried to peer in the front door, but there was a shade pulled over the window. She leaned in close, and she could hear the sound of a television's canned laughter, just vaguely. She wrapped her hand around the door handle, wondering if she should knock or just barge in.

What was going on? Was Logan inside? Was he planning to kill his uncle?

The thought spurred her to action. If she didn't act, someone would be dead.

Taking a deep breath, she twisted the handle, trying to make no noise. The mechanism gave, and the door opened.

She opened the door a crack and looked in. Seeing nothing but some hideous pink and black striped wallpaper, she pushed the door open just a little bit more. Then she slipped inside and looked around.

She crept a few steps and noticed a man, crouching in the kitchen. He had a mess of curly hair and was facing away from her, as if trying to make himself invisible. She couldn't tell what he was looking at, but it seemed as though he was peering into the living room. Watching someone. Ready to pounce.

It was him. Logan. It had to be.

She wiped her clammy hands on the front of her shorts. *Mia, you have to pounce first.* Canned laughter erupted as she took another breath, preparing to make her move.

Before she could, though, he started to turn around. She saw him in profile; pointed chin covered in stubble, pointed nose, beady eyes. In that instant, she had the brief thought that the man was a far cry from that little boy she'd seen in the picture, the one who'd been smiling with his hunting knife. But it was little more than a flash, because in the next second, he spun and lunged at her.

She expected a knife, so she was ready. She scuttled to the side, missing outstretched hands, poised to wrap around her throat, and grabbed one of his arms. It was not thin but not muscular, either. As she grabbed it, he maneuvered around her, wrenching it free and trying to wrap it around her neck, getting her into a headlock. In the blur of the moment, it struck her that he'd had both hands free. No knife.

She forced her elbow back, slamming into his ribcage. He let out a guttural moan and stumbled back against the wall. As he did, she took inventory of his form—his dark t-shirt. His baggy jeans. He was dressed like a kid, no more than twenty.

But he had no knife.

Hand out, ready to fend off another attack from him, she let her eyes slide to the side, to where he'd been crouching. She saw the remnants of something there . . . china. A broken teacup, along with brown tea, splattered on the floormat.

Wait a minute.

She turned to the man and stared at him. He wasn't attempting to fight her anymore. In fact, he just looked scared, his chest heaving as he tried to catch his breath.

When he finally did speak, still clutching at his chest, he said, "What the hell? What are you doing here?"

"Are you Logan Simmons?" she demanded.

His face wrinkled in confusion. "Logan … no. He's my cousin. I'm Connor. Connor Simmons. "

She stared at him in shock. "You weren't . . .?"

"I was making tea. For me and my dad," he said, his eyes full of disgust. "And I dropped the cup by accident."

"What's going on in there, Con?" an older male voice called from the living room.

"Nothing, Dad," the boy called out, then fixed her with a hard stare. "Look, whoever you are. I don't know what you're doing, but you've got the wrong house. Logan's living at his dad's trailer now, a few streets over. And I don't what the hell you're thinking, barging into a person's house when you're not even sure where they live."

"I'm sorry, but . . ." Her face heated, and she fumbled to come up with some excuse. The only one she could remember was the one she'd told earlier. "I'm Logan's teacher. And I'm worried about him. Have you seen him?"

He shook his head. "Get in line. We're all worried about him. But I haven't seen him in a week. He keeps to himself. Which is probably why we're all worried about him. No one can get through to him. And lately . . . lately he seems to have gone off the rails."

"What does that mean?"

Connor shrugged. "We used to hunt together, a few days every month. But he didn't even want to do that. I've called him. He ignores me."

Oh, he'd definitely gone off the rails, even more than the boy knew. Maybe Logan was here right now. Waiting for his moment. Mia moved in, trying to scan the place.

Connor flinched. "Don't come near me."

"I have reason to believe Logan's been harming his family members," she stated, feeling guilty for scaring the kid. She moved back, trying to be as unthreatening as possible.

"His family members? What makes you say that?"

"Because I just found his father, dead in his trailer," she said, losing patience.

Connor's eyes widened. "Dead? Uncle Keith? Are you—"

"Yeah. I'm sure. And to make sure you're safe I think should check your trailer to make sure—"

"Logan wouldn't do that. No way," Connor stated, crossing his arms.

"He did." She said it bluntly, leaving no room for doubt. "And he killed his own mother, too, a babysitter, and one of his other cousins. He's going after people who might have wronged him in the past, I think."

Connor shook his head fiercely. "Well, that isn't us. We never did anything to hurt him. He might've not gotten along with his parents, but he used to come over here to escape them. He wouldn't—" He paused, shaking. "How did you find our place, then? If Uncle Keith is dead and Logan's missing?"

"Everything okay in there, Con? Who're you talking to?" the voice called from the other room.

Connor didn't break Mia's gaze, his eyes still demanding an answer, but he called out, "Everything's fine, Dad. Be right there."

"His neighbor, next door, told me. So can I—"

"Smitty?" he asked, raising his eyebrow. "The guy with the shotgun?"

She paused. She hadn't gotten his name, but yes, he'd definitely had a gun. "Yes."

He snorted. "That guy's crazy. Nosy as hell. Always causing trouble, pretending to be helpful to Uncle Keith but treating Logan like shit when his father's back was turned. Logan hated living next to him."

It seemed that Logan Simmons had trouble with a lot of people. As far as she knew, his uncle was the next logical choice. Someone he knew, who'd had a part in raising him. And just because Connor thought they had a good relationship, didn't mean they actually did. "He's got to still be here. If you'll just let me take a look—"

She suddenly froze, as thoughts flooded her.

Logan hated living next to him.

Keith had custody sometimes, so I'd look in on the kid while he was growing up, try to give him advice.

Oh, he's always terrorizing Poochie, my dog. Taking his knife out and waving it at him, saying he was going to cut his heart out. So I told him this afternoon that if he tried anything like that again, I was going to report him to the police. I told him to go get a job and stop being a lowlife.

As the words funneled through her head, she thought of Merry. Merry hadn't been related to him, but she'd had a part in raising him. And the neighbor, Smitty, by checking in on him, had, too.

Connor was saying something about how if she really wanted to, she could check the place, but that he thought it would be a waste of time. When she caught the tail end of his statement, she realized she agreed with him.

And she'd made a huge mistake.

"Oh, God," she whispered, backing toward the door.

The kid's brow wrinkled. "What's wrong? Didn't you want to check—"

She turned and made a break for the door. "Not now. I have to get back to Smitty."

*

When she rounded the corner and faced the trailer that had belonged to Logan Simmons, where his father, Keith Simmons, lay dead, Mia expected all hell to be breaking loose.

But at first, everything looked calm, just as it had from the moment she'd arrived in the trailer park. She slid to an abrupt stop, the crunching of gravel underfoot giving way to the thudding of her own heartbeat. But there was no other sound. Inside Smitty's trailer, a single light glowed near the front door.

Then she heard it. Not loud, but definite.

The sound of a small dog, yipping. Poochie.

Though she'd had enough of barging into places where she wasn't welcome, she didn't have a moment to waste. She barreled up the stairs, turned the knob, and shoved open the door, bursting into the small trailer.

The sight was almost beyond belief.

The poor old man, Smitty, lying on the floor, his shotgun beside him. There was a gaping wound in his stomach. He was awake, though, panting and trying to lift himself off the ground, reaching for the gun. Poochie stood at his feet, head tossed back, yipping in alarm.

When she came in, Smitty's eyes fell on her, and he pointed, his mouth twisting into words she couldn't understand.

She finally did understand them—*Behind you*—a beat too late.

Because in that beat, a hand fell on her shoulder, and she felt the blade of the knife ripping into the back of her t-shirt.

She sprang forward, rounding on him.

"Who the hell do you think you are?" Logan Simmons snarled, his mouth dripping with saliva, his eyes almost completely covered by a long, black fringe of bangs. Wearing a tight black t-shirt that clung to his lean frame and baggy camo pants, he wielded the knife between them, swinging it, like he thought he was some samurai warrior. "This is none of your business. But I guess I'll have to kill you for getting in the way."

"I'm a friend of Merry's. And you killed her. I tracked you down. Finally."

He scoffed as he ran an eye over her. "*You're* a friend of Merry's? Are you as worthless as she is? She deserved to die. You know, she used to lock me in a closet for *hours*. Call me a terror and keep me in there, no matter how hard I banged my fists on the door. She'd only let me out when my mom came home. My stupid mom, who actually *paid* her, even though I told her what had happened."

"And so your mom had to die, too," she said, backing into the kitchenette, pushing the small of her back against the counter, near the sink.

A smile spread over his face. "You've done your homework. Good for you. Maybe you're not as stupid as them. But you're still going to end up like them."

He advanced toward her, but in the last second, she acted. She reached over, grabbed the toaster, yanked its cord from the wall, and brought it down, hard, on his head.

He let out a wail and slashed at her, the knife only hitting the fabric of her loose shirt. As the knife finished its round, she reached for it, grabbing his hand. He followed with an elbow to her chest that knocked the air out of her.

Clutching her chest, she backed up, only to tangle herself in his legs. She lost balance and fell backwards, pain screaming up her spine as her back hit the hard tile floor. Her head cracked against the cabinets, sending her vision spinning.

Before she could collect herself enough to get up, he stepped in front of her. She heard the heavy footsteps, this low laughter, as she looked up. Through her bleary eyes, she watched the shadow of him raise his knife high above her, ready to plunge it into her chest.

"Get ready to die," he hissed out, grinning widely, and she braced herself.

Before he could bring it down, though, behind him, the door swung open. Logan didn't have time to turn. A single gunshot rang out, and his smile disappeared from his face, replaced by only shock. He spun slightly, then slumped to the ground.

In his place stood her former partner, David Hunter.

If she wasn't mistaken, the U.S. Marshals would be right behind.

But right now, as she lay sprawled out on the cold kitchen tile, exhausted and aching, she didn't even care.

CHAPTER THIRTY

Mia sat up, clutching her head, trying to force her eyes to focus and stretch her sore back muscles. Each time she blinked, her vision came closer to normal. And as she stretched, her body hurt less and less. Nothing broken or bleeding, it seemed.

But she had bigger problems on her hands right now.

As she stared at the form of Logan Simmons, lying at her feet, David came in, crouched in front of him, and checked his pulse. Then he pulled his phone out of his pocket. “You okay?” he asked her, as the form of U.S. Marshal Kane Wilcox filled the doorway, blocking any possible exit.

She didn’t know how to answer that question. Yes, her physical wounds would heal.

But right now, mentally, she was far from okay.

Visions of possible futures plagued her—going off to prison, hearing her daughter crying on the other end of the phone, growing old away from her family. Nausea tangled her gut. She didn’t have the strength to try to escape again. And so that meant that she’d failed. Not just herself, but her family, and everyone who had ever believed in her on this long journey to expose the truth.

“Yeah, David Hunter from the FBI. I need an ambulance here at Wild Texas Trailer Park, we’ve got a man stabbed and a man shot,” David barked into the phone, stepping into the living room where the old man was. As he disappeared from view, Kane Wilcox stepped forward.

He wasn’t smiling in triumph, relishing his villain’s, *So, Mia North, we finally meet face-to-face* moment. In fact, his face was a straight line, which surprised her. He ran an eye over her, appraising her, as if he’d expected something a lot more formidable. She got it—crumpled in the corner of the kitchen, she wasn’t exactly at her best.

Still, he should’ve had a little bit of pride in this accomplishment. He’d been after her for the better part of two months, after all. But it was almost as if he was disappointed that he’d finally caught up with her.

She said, "Well, Agent. You caught me. Aren't you going to gloat?"

He shook his head slowly, then dragged a hand down his face. "Is that what you thought I'd do?"

She tried to shrug, but that hurt too much. She'd hit her back hard. Instead, she flexed her spine. Better. "Pretty much."

He walked toward her and offered her a hand to help her up. She stared at it like it was infected. When he realized she wasn't going to take it, he grabbed a chair from the kitchen set and faced it toward her. Sitting in it, he said, "Then I guess you thought wrong."

"I'm impressed by your restraint," she said, motioning with her chin toward the living room, where David was still speaking with the 911 operator. "Which is more than I can say for your new partner, over there."

A slight twinge of amusement appeared on his face. "He's *your* partner."

"Not anymore," she spat out.

He shifted in his chair. "No, I think you're wrong about that. Maybe he's not your partner on the official books, and maybe you felt he betrayed you during that trial, and I wouldn't blame you for that. But I think he's more than redeemed himself."

She tilted her head. "In *your* eyes, maybe." She was tired of this conversation. If she was going to be brought in, she might as well get it over with. She held her wrists out to him, ready to feel the cold metal clink around them. "Go ahead."

He shook his head. "I'm not here to arrest you, Mia."

She stared, confused. That couldn't be possible. He surely wasn't here to give her a thank you. He hadn't been chasing after her all this time to let her go like some too-small fish. So then . . . what was his game? "What?"

He settled back into the chair, as comfortably as if he was sitting to watch a football game, crossing one leg over the other so that the ankle was on his knee. "David Hunter tells me you think you were framed. So I've spent a long time looking into your case. . . and I tend to believe you."

She stared at him for a long time. "Tend to?"

"Enough so that I'm risking my job by not bringing you in right now." When she didn't say anything, uncrossed his legs and dropped the foot, heavy, to the floor, leaning forward. "And I think as a former

Fed yourself, you know what a big risk that is. Uncle Sam isn't exactly the most forgiving of employers."

Mia knew that well. Being a Federal Agent came with all the red tape one would expect—rules upon rules, some seemingly nonsensical, but all of them rigid and unbreakable. And doing this, telling her what he was, now? He wasn't just risking his own job. He could be thrown in jail himself, for a very long time.

She pulled her knees up to her chest. "Okay, so what *do* you believe, Agent?"

"I believe that you didn't have a fair trial. That the facts were twisted in a way to make you look guilty. And that the evidence didn't show conclusively that you were the one who killed Ellis Horvath. Which means I don't believe you should've gone to prison," he said.

She couldn't help it. She laughed. "Can you tell your boss that? And your boss's boss? And whoever else needs to know so that they'll clear me?"

"It's not as easy as that," he said, shaking his head. "I'm going to need time to get things together and accumulate the evidence that's going to be needed to prove the case. But I want you to know, I'm looking into it."

She blurted out the first thing that came to her mind. "Can you look into it *fast*?"

He raised an eyebrow. Then he said, "I get it. You're tired of running. Anyone would be."

She nodded, feeling every one of those past days she'd spent, on the lam, hit her like a ton of bricks. She hadn't had one relaxing day in ages. A thought came to her of the last one—she and her family, Aiden, Kelsey, her parents and sister Francine, out on the back deck, having a barbecue. Stupidly, she'd left that fun time in a hurry, to deal with the phone call that had gotten her in trouble in the first place. If she could just go back in time . . . if she had just waited for David's backup, or better yet, not gone at all, everything would've been different.

David came in at that moment. "Hey, Mia. We know you're probably suffering."

Probably? She almost laughed. "I've thought about turning myself in every minute for the past three weeks. Of just putting an end to this," she admitted honestly.

"We know," Hunter said, leaning against the wall. "But just a little longer. Promise me. If you want to be back with your family and get your record cleared, then you have to trust that we're doing it as fast as we can. Keep the faith, and don't stop running."

She nodded, wondering how she ever doubted him in the first place.

"But Mia . . ." he started, causing her eyes to flash to his. He leaned in and spoke in a deeper, much more serious voice. "Try to lay low and keep a low profile, would you?"

She had to smile at his exasperation. She had been tempting fate. She knew that. But solving cases was in her blood. She couldn't simply stop, no matter what her circumstances. "But I—"

"No buts. You keep coming into the belly of the beast, you're gonna get yourself digested."

She let out a laugh, her first laugh in a long time. "I'll try."

Just then, there were sirens. The ambulance. Wilcox jumped to his feet, and David looked out the door. "The police are here," he said quickly, motioning her up. "You have to go."

Still a little woozy, she pulled herself up to standing, hardly believing his words. Her eyes went from Hunter to Wilcox, waiting for one of them to pull the rug out from under her. "You're really just letting me go?"

"That's right."

David Hunter held the door open for her. "Let's go."

She moved forward. No, she didn't have the strength to think of another escape plan. But this time, miraculously, she didn't have to escape. They were letting her go. As she forced her legs to move, she realized she *did* have the strength to run, especially knowing she had allies, more people on her side than she'd thought.

She could do this.

And she *would* do this.

If it meant that her name would be cleared and she could be back with her family again, she'd do whatever it took.

As she stepped to the door, he handed her a stuffed drawstring bag. "Necessities. Take care, North."

She looked inside to find what looked like some clothing, and nodded at him. "Thank you."

The lights of the police cars bounced off of the surface of nearby trailers, and the sirens ripped through the quiet of night, closer and louder. She stepped onto the gravel and made her way down the lane, away from the commotion, and when she reached the edge of the park, broke into a run and stole out into the night.

EPILOGUE

Mia spent the next two days lying low in a campsite south of Dallas, close to Irving. It was remote, and quiet, and allowed her to recuperate from the excitement of the Logan Simmons case.

But two days was more than enough.

Mia never had been good at waiting. Now, she was antsy.

She'd spent most of that time, thinking about her conversation with David and Kane Wilcox, wondering if what they said was actually true. Obviously, she believed them now—they wouldn't have let her go, otherwise. But could Kane Wilcox really help her? Look into things on her behalf? Bring the killer to justice? And best of all, make her a free woman?

As incredible as all that sounded, she still had hope.

So after two days, body healed and energy renewed, she was chomping at the bit for news of any small development in their research.

And there was only way to get in touch with them.

That was why, after those two days, she gathered up the meager belongings David had given her—a toiletry kit, a few changes of clothes, and some cash—into the small drawstring bag it had come in, and hitched her way up to University Park.

She found a trucker who would drive her most of the way, so she only had to walk the last mile. Instead of draining her, though, her excitement increased with every step.

But so did her anxiety. This was University Park, where she'd once lived, crawling with police. When she got to the auto body shop where she'd always exchanged messages with David, she took a deep breath, checking over her shoulder every two seconds as she approached the key-drop.

Kane Wilcox had said he would help her, but that didn't mean every other law enforcement officer in Dallas didn't want her head. It had made her an incredibly paranoid person. Mia had to wonder if, free woman or not, she'd spend the rest of her life, checking over her shoulder, out of pure force of habit.

But right now, she didn't mind it so much. Those two days had done her good. That, and the knowledge that not only had David not betrayed her, but that he'd called in help. And that she had another soul she could trust. It gave her the small indication that maybe her escape wasn't for nothing. Maybe her plan to stay out of jail and prove her own innocence was working. Maybe, with enough time and effort, she could swerve so many people over to her side that opinion would tip in her favor, and she could be pardoned.

It was a long shot. But it was also the only hope she had.

And now, because of David Hunter, it was growing. It wasn't a light at the end of the tunnel just yet . . . but it was something.

When she stepped in front of the key drop, she said a little prayer that there was some good news in there. A new witness. An attorney reviewing the case for evidence of a mistrial. Wilson Andrews, breaking down and admitting he'd had her framed (okay, that one was a *really* long shot). She opened the metal flap and dipped her hand in, then pulled out a single, folded sheet of paper. On the front of it, it said, simply, M.

She opened it up and read:

M,

Be at the place of the Hunter case at 4pm Thursday for a surprise.

D

She stared at it, knowing exactly what it meant, as if it had all been written there in black and white for her. The Hunter case was one of the first cases they'd solved, where a kid, Ian Hunter, had been taken from a giant wooden castle playground in the hours of dusk. It was thought to be related to another case, earlier, where a child had been murdered, so the FBI was called in. But after some investigation, he'd been found, unhurt, a block away. He'd followed the sound of an ice cream truck and had gotten lost. False alarm.

So that meant Farrington Park. And the surprise? Well, it could've been anything, even a man standing there with her official pardon. But that, though it would be amazing, wasn't what she was hoping for.

She hadn't seen her family in so long. Maybe he'd arranged a short visit?

She wouldn't have to wait long. Today was Thursday, and the meeting was arranged for later that afternoon. In her excitement, she ran out right away to hitch another ride and made it there an hour ahead of time.

It was later in the day, and too hot, so the park was pretty empty. As she sat on a bench with her hoodie pulled up around her face despite the sweltering temperatures, she felt tears being pulled from her eyes whenever a little girl ran past, squealing in glee. It reminded her too much of her own daughter.

So she busied herself by reading a book that David had also given her—*The Count of Monte Cristo* by Alexander Dumas. Turned out, Hunter had a sense of humor when it came to his reading choices for her.

But when she looked up briefly and saw them like an oasis across the playground, she couldn't do anything but stare, drinking in all of their individual characteristics as they came into view.

It was her daughter and her husband, walking toward her.

Her heart sped up as she watched them cross the playground, smiling at her. Kelsey's wide grin every much a child's, the one Mia had come to love, glowing with unencumbered glee. But there was pain behind Aiden's happy expression. It looked like he was doing his best to hold things together, for his daughter's sake.

When there were just a few steps between them, Kelsey screamed, "Mommy!" and broke into a run, throwing herself into Mia's arms.

Mia took in her smell, the tickle of her hair on her face, the way she no longer fit into her arms as a compact eight-year-old. Now, she was different, and yet, it was the same Kelsey, her same little girl that she'd thought of, every moment of every day since she'd been born.

"Hey, baby," she said, smoothing the girl's hair back, tears coming to her own eyes. "Oh, it's so good to see you. I thought I might--"

"When are you coming home?" Kelsey asked, her eyes full of hope.

She glanced at Aiden, then leaned in and gave him a kiss. "We're working on it," she said, hoping he'd say more. After all, David Hunter had to have contacted him. Maybe he'd have more information on the progress of their investigation. But he simply pulled her into a tight hug.

"We've missed you."

They hugged together for a long time, and Mia looked at Kelsey, seeing how much she'd grown—at least a couple inches, and her hair was lighter now. Aiden still hadn't been able to figure out how to properly do her hair, but she looked happy and healthy, all things considered. They squeezed onto the bench together, Kelsey chattering on about everything going on in fourth grade.

After Mia listened to the rundown, wishing she could be there for every moment of it, Kelsey said, "Mom, let me show you a cool trick I learned in gymnastics," and ran off to the monkey bars.

"Did David talk to you?" she asked softly as she watched Kelsey climb and do a flip over the bars. She clapped her hands. "Wow! That's great Kels!"

"Not really. He just told me to meet you here. So I did," he said with a shrug. "What's going on?"

She sighed. "Things are in motion, I think. At least, I hope. I have David and another federal agent looking into my case. They believe me, and think they can bring me home."

He looked at her. "How? You've been convicted of murder. Unless they find the person who did it—"

"Bingo."

He raised an eyebrow. "You know who did it?"

"Well, no, I don't know exactly who did it. But I think it was a hit. And I think the person who ordered it is Wilson Andrews."

Horror dawned on his face. "You still think that he's involved? That he did this?"

"Oh, he's involved up to his eyeballs. I just have to find some way to prove it."

He shook his head. "Mia, if he's behind it, you might as well call yourself screwed."

She tilted her head. "What do you mean?"

"Mommy! Look at this!" Kelsey called from the slide.

Mia turned to her and cheered. "Really great! Wow!"

Aiden's voice was now lacking any excitement at all. Instead, it was quiet and serious. "He owns this city. This *state*. The police love him, the teachers love him, the press loves him. He can do no wrong. That's why when his brother got arrested after that serial killing thing, it didn't even show on his record. He's untouchable."

She frowned. She'd wanted him to cheer her up, to encourage her. And now, he was doing the opposite. "Yes, but—"

"He's not only untouchable, he's dangerous."

"Maybe, but—"

"But—what I don't understand is why, if you think he's behind all this, you're sticking around. You need to go, Meem. You need to get out of here. Go to Mexico."

She stared at him in horror. "Don't be silly. I can't just leave you—"

"Don't you get it? You need to leave. You're accusing him of doing some really dirty things. He'll stop at nothing to shut you up. If you start meddling with Wilson Andrews, you're putting all of us in danger. Don't you see?" He scanned the area. "It's a danger for us to even be here now."

"No," she said, reaching for his hand, but he stood up and stalked to the edge of the playground.

"Kelsey!" he barked, and she immediately put her head up. "Come on. Time to go."

"But Daddy, I need to—"

"*Now.*"

Mia had never heard him use a voice like that. Aiden was quiet, mild-mannered. But he used force and voice when he needed to. When it mattered. And this mattered. His voice told her just how serious this was. Once he got something in his head, he never backed down. So she knew nothing she said would deter him.

Still, she couldn't bear the thought of him leaving, after so many nights and days spent, wishing to be near them again. Especially on these terms. "Aiden, it's okay, it's—"

"It's not, Mia." She'd never heard him this angry. He opened his wallet, pulled out some hundreds, and handed the bills to her. When she didn't take them, he shoved them into her arms. "Take this. Go. Go over the border to Mexico. Get out. And don't contact us again."

Don't contact us again. Was that even possible? Did he really want that?

She tried to look into his eyes, to calm him, to tell him it was all right. But he wouldn't meet hers. Fifteen years of being together, of being each other's best, closest friend, were gone in an instant.

"Aiden," she whispered, hardly able to believe this was happening. That this happy moment could be destroyed in an instant.

But it was happening, and there was nothing Mia had in her power to stop it. She watched helplessly as Aiden marched over to Kelsey and took her by the hand, whirling her around and pointing her toward the parking lot. "Mommy! Bye!" she called over her shoulder in a fragile-as-glass voice, a little confused as they walked off, toward their car.

She turned around every so often, still waving, her big brown eyes sad, as if even the little girl knew that she'd never see her mother again.

Wait, one more kiss. One more hug, she wanted to call out.

But he was right. Aiden usually was. He always did what was best for the family. She was being selfish, wanting to see them, putting them in danger. So while this might not have been the best thing for her—in fact, it felt like an arrow shot straight through her heart—it was the best thing for all of them.

Mia waved at Kelsey as her face blurred into the distance, forcing her feet to stay rooted to her spot, even as the thing she wanted most of all slipped from her grip.

Her husband, however, never looked back.

As she stood there, watching and hoping they would return, feeling more and more helpless, a hand fell on her shoulder.

It was David Hunter.

"Come on," he said. "It's time to get to work."

NOW AVAILABLE!

<u>SEE HER DEAD</u>
(A Mia North FBI Suspense Thriller—Book 6)

When a series of mysterious murders leaves the FBI stumped, the FBI secretly needs fugitive FBI Agent Mia North's help to use her former connections in the penal system. But Mia must walk a treacherous line as she seeks to crack the case—and keep herself from going back to jail—as she walks right into a direct confrontation with the U.S. Marshal on her trail.

"A brilliant book. I couldn't put it down and I never guessed who the murderer was!"
—Reader review for Only Murder

Special Agent Mia North is a rising star in the FBI—until, in an elaborate setup, she's framed for murder and sentenced to prison. When a lucky break allows her to escape, Mia finds herself a fugitive, on the run and on the wrong side of the law for the first time in her life. She can't see her young daughter—and she has no hope of returning to her former life.

The only way to get her life back, she realizes, is to hunt down whoever framed her.

An action-packed page-turner, the MIA NORTH series is a riveting crime thriller, jammed with suspense, surprises, and twists and turns that you won't see coming. Fall in love with this brilliant new female protagonist and you'll be turning pages late into the night.

Future books in this series will be available soon.

"I loved this thriller, read it in one sitting. Lots of twists and turns and I didn't guess the

culprit at all… Already pre-ordered the second!"
—Reader review for Only Murder

"This book takes off with a bang… An excellent read, and I'm looking forward to the next book!"
—Reader review for SEE HER RUN

"Fantastic book! It was hard to put down. I can't wait to see what happens next!"
—Reader review for SEE HER RUN

"The twists and turns kept coming. Can't wait to read the next book!"
—Reader review for SEE HER RUN

"A must-read if you enjoy action-packed stories with good plots!"
—Reader review for SEE HER RUN

"I really like this author and this series starts with a bang. It will keep you turning the pages till the end of the book and wanting more."
—Reader review for SEE HER RUN

"I can't say enough about this author! How about 'out of this world'! This author is going to go far!"
—Reader review for ONLY MURDER

"I really enjoyed this book… The characters were alive, and the twists and turns were great. It will keep you reading till the end and leave you wanting more."
—Reader review for NO WAY OUT

"This is an author that I highly recommend. Her books will have you begging for more."
—Reader review for NO WAY OUT

Rylie Dark

Bestselling author Rylie Dark is author of the SADIE PRICE FBI SUSPENSE THRILLER series, comprising six books (and counting); the MIA NORTH FBI SUSPENSE THRILLER series, comprising six books (and counting); the CARLY SEE FBI SUSPENSE THRILLER, comprising six books (and counting); and the MORGAN STARK FBI SUSPENSE THRILLER, comprising three books (and counting).

An avid reader and lifelong fan of the mystery and thriller genres, Rylie loves to hear from you, so please feel free to visit www.ryliedark.com to learn more and stay in touch.

BOOKS BY RYLIE DARK

SADIE PRICE FBI SUSPENSE THRILLER
ONLY MURDER (Book #1)
ONLY RAGE (Book #2)
ONLY HIS (Book #3)
ONLY ONCE (Book #4)
ONLY SPITE (Book #5)
ONLY MADNESS (Book #6)

MIA NORTH FBI SUSPENSE THRILLER
SEE HER RUN (Book #1)
SEE HER HIDE (Book #2)
SEE HER SCREAM (Book #3)
SEE HER VANISH (Book #4)
SEE HER GONE (Book #5)
SEE HER DEAD (Book #6)

CARLY SEE FBI SUSPENSE THRILLER
NO WAY OUT (Book #1)
NO WAY BACK (Book #2)
NO WAY HOME (Book #3)
NO WAY LEFT (Book #4)
NO WAY UP (Book #5)
NO WAY TO DIE (Book #6)

MORGAN STARK FBI SUSPENSE THRILLER
TOO LATE (Book #1)
TOO CLOSE (Book #2)
TOO FAR GONE (Book #3)

www.ingramcontent.com/pod-product-compliance
Lightning Source LLC
Chambersburg PA
CBHW030615310726
48979CB00003B/723

* 9 7 8 1 0 9 4 3 9 5 5 8 6 *